> ## "I'm afraid you're going to have to inform the bride the marriage is off!"

Jack rubbed his temples. How had this happened to him? "This is all too much to take in," he said wearily. He was about to say more but the sound of the door opening caught his attention. The bride stepped inside and looked at her husband quizzically.

"Darling, people are going to think you've abandoned me before the wedding cake is cut." She looped her arm through Jack's, keeping an eye on Cassandra. "And who is this?"

Jack didn't know whether to die right then and there or just confess the truth. For a man used to quiet academia, he was in way over his head. He opened his mouth to say something when Casey cut him off.

"I'm Jack's...sister," she said, punctuating the last word with a searing look at him.

The bride smiled. "Jack never told me he had a sister. I do hope we'll get a chance to get to know each other better." She lifted her champagne glass in a toast.

Casey did the same. "I'd like that. I've a feeling we have a great deal in common."

ABOUT THE AUTHOR

Linda Randall Wisdom knew she was destined to write romance novels when her first sale came on her wedding anniversary. Careers in personnel, marketing and public relations have fed the imagination of this creative full-time writer who has penned over fifty books. Her trademark zany humor has made her a reader favorite. Linda was recently named one of the top ten favorite romance writers by *Affaire de Coeur* readers. She lives in Southern California with her husband and a houseful of exotic pets.

Books by Linda Randall Wisdom

HARLEQUIN AMERICAN ROMANCE

Linda Randall Wisdom

MR. & MRS.... & MRS.?

Harlequin Books

TORONTO • NEW YORK • LONDON
AMSTERDAM • PARIS • SYDNEY • HAMBURG
STOCKHOLM • ATHENS • TOKYO • MILAN
MADRID • WARSAW • BUDAPEST • AUCKLAND

A thank-you for the "pure and good" Alison Hart for her sparkling idea. One day I will lead you into complete writer's corruption. I promise. <G>

ISBN 0-373-16681-8

MR. & MRS....& MRS.?

Copyright © 1997 by Words by Wisdom.

Printed in U.S.A.

Prologue

"Is going on this expedition such a good idea, Cassandra? It isn't as if you don't have work here, and I've read the Amazon can be dangerous if you don't have the right guides and equipment."

Dr. Cassandra Daniels-Larson looked up from the canvas duffel bag she was stuffing to the bursting point with twill trousers, shorts and cotton shirts. Her light brown hair was neatly combed back in its usual twist, and her glasses constantly threatened to slide down her pert nose. She used her forefinger to push her glasses back up. At the same time, she lifted her head to gaze at her husband as he stood next to her.

"You didn't even discuss the full extent of this expedition with me," he added in an even tone that didn't betray the feelings he had locked inside. Anyone looking at him would have thought he was discussing nothing more serious than the weather.

Jonathon Larson looked like the philosophy professor he was. Tortoise-rimmed glasses surrounded dark green eyes and rusty brown hair clipped short as befitting his position in the small but prestigious university he and his wife were a part of. His white shirt looked as if wrinkles dared not mar the soft cloth and his trousers were equally well pressed. Right now, his pleasant-looking features were slightly furrowed in a thoughtful frown.

"Of course I talked about this opportunity with you, Jonathon. I told you about it in great detail. The university thinks it's a wonderful chance for me, and besides, I'll only be gone for eighteen months." Cassandra's calm voice refused to rise a decibel. "This is a fantastic opportunity I can't even think of giving up. Think of the papers I should be able to publish. We will be meeting tribes who will be receiving modern medical care for the first time in their lives."

Her voice became animated as she spoke of the new experiences in her chosen field. More animated than it ever sounded when they made love, Jonathon thought morosely as he studied her face. What would it take to drag his wife out of her self-involved world and show her there's more to life than medicine? At the same time, what would it take for him to make his way up to her level, to achieve as much as she had? He sadly wondered if the next fifty years would be sufficient for his quest. After all, his wife was a genius who had graduated medical school at the age of seventeen and had more degrees than a person knew what to do with. No wonder there were times he felt below her notice.

He watched her double-check her list against items packed in the two bags.

"We'll have the medical supplies brought in by boat," she said, more to herself than to her husband. "Greg said news of this unknown tribe rocked his entire team. To be asked to accompany them is an honor," she said.

Jonathon sighed. "Cassandra, I'm not sure this is a good time for you to go," he began, still wondering how to tell her that sometimes he felt as if their marriage wasn't all it was supposed to be. That there had to be more. He didn't want to end it, but what was so wrong with a wife preferring to stay with her husband than traipse off to the Amazon jungle where anything could happen?

Cassandra looked at him with the same bland smile she always had. "It's not as if we won't be in contact. There will be mail delivery, although I think not on a regular basis." She looked around. "Now, did I forget anything?" She tapped her forefinger against her chin as she mentally ran through her list again.

He swallowed another sigh as he picked up her bags and followed her to the front door. Cassandra had dissuaded him from driving her to the airport since Greg had offered to pick her up. She said there was no sense in wasting gas. When she was acting practical, no one had a chance.

Cassandra offered him a bright smile as she kissed him lightly on the lips.

"Goodbye, Jonathon. And don't worry about me."

She patted his shoulder. "Before you know it, the eighteen months will be up and we'll have our lives in order again." She waved to the dark blue van that had rolled into the driveway.

Jonathon stood on the porch watching the van pull away. He noticed once Dr. Greg Matthews started talking, Cassandra was more interested in whatever he had to say than to take one last look at her husband.

"Yes, you forgot something," he muttered, walking back into the house. "You forgot me."

Chapter One

"I have to say it isn't all that easy tracking down your husband, Dr. Daniels-Larson." A man dressed in a naval uniform walked into the room.

Cassandra, seated on the bed, looked up at the man's entrance. "I can't understand why not. This is the middle of the third quarter. He'd have to be at the university."

The captain shook his head. "I'm sorry, Doctor, but the university said he hasn't been on their faculty for two years. Now, I—"

"What?" Cassandra jumped off the bed, cutting off the captain's explanation. "That can't be!"

"Now, Doctor," he said tentatively, "we do have someone trying to trace your husband's whereabouts. As soon as we track him down, we'll contact him with the news of your rescue."

"Actually, Captain, I'd rather surprise him." Cassandra combed her fingers through her hair, which

hung in heavy waves way past her shoulders. Thanks to all the days under the hot tropical sun, her hair had lightened to a combination of bronze and blond that artfully highlighted her deep golden tanned skin. Her case of sunblock had run out after the first seven months, and after everything that had happened, the threat of skin cancer hadn't scared her. In fact, in the last few years, she'd had the chance to have many an internal dialogue with herself and to think about her marriage in ways she hadn't thought about before....
What she'd come to realize was that she needed to make a great many apologies to her husband. In fact, now that she was back in civilization, she intended to make a great many changes. Starting with herself. She thought about the obscenely large check the foundation had sent her. Guilt for losing her and the rest of the team in the Amazon for more than three years turned out to be very expensive. She smiled as she thought of all that money could buy.

"I was thinking that while you try to find my husband, I would have the chance to do a little shopping and catch up with life," she said, hopping off the bed. "No offense to you, Captain, but do you happen to have a woman around here who would have something more stylish than a dress uniform?" She picked up the check and waved it in the air.

He grinned. "I guess I should introduce you to my wife. There's nothing she enjoys more than shopping. She'll be happy to help you spend your money."

"JACK, ARE YOU ALL RIGHT?"

He turned at the sound of the low, sultry voice belonging to his fiancée, Nan Xavier. Dressed in a clinging red silk sheath that bared her shoulders, she would have looked like the perfect picture of a vamp if it hadn't been for her warm smile. Inside the country club's main ballroom, a Glenn Miller tune was playing in the background for those who wished to dance.

"Oh, no, you're not allowed to have second thoughts," she teased, gliding over to him and curving her arm through his, lifting her face for his kiss. "If you think you can escape, you are very wrong. And I will kidnap you until the ceremony tomorrow afternoon if I have to."

"Depends where you take me," he teased back.

Nan squeezed his arm. "You are a very wonderful man to do this for me," she said softly.

He smiled. "Considering the way Norton planned this, I guess neither one of us had a chance. There's nothing like a man lying in a hospital bed to make you feel you have to do everything possible to ensure the remainder of his life is peaceful."

"Think of it as doing your good deed for the century," she told him. "Daddy is in there tonight looking better than I've seen him since before his heart attack." Her smile dimmed for a moment. "I'm just grateful you were willing to accede to his wishes."

"All right, you two, why aren't you inside enjoying your own engagement party?" A man's voice boomed from nearby. "Couples only have one, you know."

Nan's face brightened as she turned to face the intruder. "Now, Daddy, perhaps we wanted to enjoy our party out here," she quipped, walking over and hugging the older man.

Jack studied his prospective father-in-law, noting his heightened color and broad smile. For a man who'd suffered a heart attack two months ago, Norton Xavier was rapidly on the mend. A little under six feet, the man radiated the power he'd been known for as the driving force behind Xavier Electronics for more than forty years. His black tuxedo was a perfect foil for his silver hair and deep tan courtesy of days spent on the golf course.

"We're just taking a break from all the festivities," Jack explained.

"I'll go in and leave you two to talk." Nan patted her father's arm and she looked at Jack. "As for you, don't spend too much time out here. I want another dance with you."

Norton watched Nan walk back inside, stopping every so often to speak to someone. He turned back to Jack.

"You're making me a happy man, Jack," he announced. "The doctors haven't given me a lot of time, but it makes me feel easier knowing my little girl will be well taken care of. And my company, likewise, in good hands."

"You know, Nan can run the company just about as well as you can," Jack pointed out.

Norton shook his head. "No, the business world isn't for her. I want her to do what she does best."

"Take care of the house, plan parties and be a decoration," Jack muttered.

"Exactly!" he said enthusiastically, not noticing Jack's sarcasm. He slapped Jack on the back. "See you inside." He walked back in.

Jack nodded. Once he was alone, he absently patted his tuxedo breast pocket, then remembered. He had quit smoking two years ago.

There were a lot of things Jack Larson didn't do anymore. Here, no one called him Dr. Larson or Jonathon. He was Jack Larson—who might have a doctorate in philosophy but now didn't make use of it. Contact lenses replaced the glasses, twill and denim replaced the tweedy look, and he even had a tan because he'd discovered he enjoyed playing tennis and indulging in a few other outdoor sports.

After the news of Cassandra's death, Jack had refused to believe it. He had sat in his study, surrounded by textbooks and tomes of heavy philosophy and eventually came to terms with the fact that his wife wasn't coming back to him. After that, he decided he couldn't stay in the small house they'd started their marriage in. He sold it, resigned from the university and took off to find himself.

Ironically, it was here in this trendy beach town that he found a new side to himself. And it was here he met Norton Xavier and, ultimately, his daughter Nan. The two introduced him to others and before Jack realized it, he was finding himself living again. Norton even put him to work at his company, and Jack discovered big business had a challenge he hadn't appreciated before. When the older man was hospitalized with a heart attack that almost proved fatal, Jack was quickly at his bedside. What Jack hadn't expected was Norton's feeble request that Jack marry his daughter, so he would know she was well taken care of. Norton assured him Nan would make him an excellent wife, and if Jack wanted to do anything for him, to please do this. Jack hadn't thought of marrying again, but he found himself helpless to refuse the older man's request. It was the least Jack could do to ease the last days of the old man's life, especially since Norton had given Jack a whole new life. Now, seeing Norton's miraculous recovery, Jack knew he'd made the right choice.

Of course, Nan's reassurances had helped a bit, too. "I know Daddy practically emotionally blackmailed you into this proposal," she had told him. "I just want you to know how much I appreciate this and to say that if things don't work out between us, we can always dissolve the marriage after—well, after. I understand how much your wife meant to you, so there's no reason to rush into it all, is there?"

Jack had been surprised by Nan's candor, and he was also grateful. He had told her about his marriage and his wife's death but hadn't gone into great detail.

Especially not the guilt. The guilt he carried in not speaking bluntly to Cassandra before she left. Perhaps if they had had a chance to sit down and truly talk, things might have been different. Now he'd never know.

"Cassandra, I'm sorry we never had a chance to see if we were meant to remain together," he said softly, raising his champagne glass in a silent toast.

"WHAT DO YOU MEAN he resigned from the university?" Cassandra's voice rose shrilly.

The lieutenant chosen to give her the news shifted uneasily under the fury sparking in her eyes. For a moment, he was afraid that fire was going to flash out and consume him.

The lovely woman, albeit more than a little scruffy, who had arrived at the base a couple weeks ago, had noticeably improved, thanks to Marge, the captain's wife, and the nearby shopping malls. She wasted no time in getting a new wardrobe and having a few beauty treatments. Her hair had been cut short into many layers that shone with bronze-and-gold highlights whenever her head moved. Makeup highlighted tawny golden brown eyes, and the tangerine silk tank top and matching pants revealed a very fit body that no man could miss.

The young man swallowed. "Yes, ma'am. The professor moved out to West Beach...just north of San Diego," he explained. "He works for an electronics corporation as some kind of consultant."

Cassandra frowned. "A consultant? He knows nothing about electronics. Why would Jonathon leave the university?" she murmured. "He considered the campus his home away from home. He even hated to go on vacation unless it had something to do with his studies."

"It must be quite a switch from lecturing bored students," Marge commented from her comfortable perch on the couch. After her and Cassandra's first meeting, she had invited the younger woman to stay with her and the captain while Cassandra awaited word on her husband. The two had quickly become good friends and enjoyed their time together as Cassandra caught up on the past three years. "From what I've heard, West Beach is a pretty ritzy area."

Cassandra shook her head, unable to believe what she was hearing. "It doesn't make any sense," she said to herself.

"Is there anything else I can do, ma'am?" the lieutenant asked nervously.

"No, Lieutenant Parks, you've helped us quite enough," Marge spoke up, offering the young man a smile.

He nodded stiffly and placed a sheet of paper on the nearby table. "This has all the details," he muttered before taking his leave.

Marge walked over to the table and picked up the paper, scanning the page.

"Wait a minute." She hurried back to the couch and retrieved the newspaper from the coffee table.

She scanned each page until she found what she was looking for. "I knew I'd seen that name somewhere!" She held up the newspaper.

"What is it?" Cassandra walked over and looked over her shoulder. Her eyes widened to the size of dinner plates as the words she read sunk in. "How dare he think of getting married when he's still married to me!"

THE WEDDING CEREMONY and reception displayed all the elegance money could buy. The bride's gown was custom-designed for her by one of Paris's leading designers and flowers were flown in from all over the world to create a fairyland atmosphere. The father of the bride made sure everything ran smooth as clockwork.

Cassandra looked around at her surroundings, noting the opulence of the country club's ballroom as she entered the room on the arm of a naval commander who had volunteered to be her escort. They had made sure to arrive after the reception line had broken up. She didn't want her first meeting with Jonathon to be in the midst of people. She had tried to contact him by phone the past two days but was unable to reach him, and she had been unsure about leaving a message. Now she wished she had. The timing was definitely very wrong.

"I'd like to thank you, Ben, for finding a way in here for me," she told him as he snagged two champagne glasses from a waiter and handed one of the glasses to her.

"Xavier Electronics has quite a few military contracts. They like to keep us happy, and I was pleased to be of service," he replied, clinking his glass against hers. He made a face. "Even if it means wearing the full dress uniform."

"And here you look so handsome in it," she teased, even as her gaze was wandering through the room looking for the bride and groom. It wasn't long before she found the happy couple. Her smile froze on her lips.

A silver-haired man in a black tuxedo stood up with a glass of champagne held high in his hand.

"To my daughter Nan and her husband Jack," he announced. "May they take Xavier Electronics into the next century for their children to run." He chuckled as many of the guests laughed appreciatively. He turned to Jack. "You have my only daughter, Jack. Take good care of her."

"I will, sir," he said solemnly.

"To Jack and Nan," the best man next announced in a loud voice, lifting his glass in a toast. "It will be interesting to see what they do bring into the next century!"

"Jack?" Cassandra muttered under the cover of surrounding laughter, now more confused than ever. "He calls himself Jack now?"

"It has been used as a shorter version of Jonathon," Ben commented in a low voice.

"He hates nicknames," she continued in a voice that didn't bode well for the man she was staring at. "He always said they were an abomination of a person's name. I was called Casey while I was growing up and he never liked it. He always called me Cassandra." Her eyes narrowed to dangerous slits. A temper she never had before was starting to appear. "This is a farce."

"So why didn't we show up for the ceremony, where you could have stood up and explained why he couldn't get married?" Ben asked.

She took a deep breath. "I guess I had hoped it was the wrong Jonathon Larson." She grabbed Ben's free hand and pulled him through the crowd until they stood off to the side, where they were in perfect view of the groom and where she could see him. She wanted to make sure there was no mistake when her husband looked this way and saw his wife. His *first* and *only* wife.

JACK LAUGHED AT SOME of the ridiculous toasts, but he obligingly drank to each and every one. His smile abruptly dimmed when he turned his head and saw a woman standing next to a man in a naval uniform. He almost choked on the champagne he was drinking. He shook his head to clear the buzz, but it didn't help. He even closed his eyes and opened them again, positive the champagne was causing what had to be nothing more than a figment of his imagination.

It couldn't be! She looked like Cassandra, but she

couldn't be. Cassandra would never have worn a dress so sleek, so, so...short. He told himself he was only imagining seeing her because he had thought of her that morning as he got ready. As he realized he was starting a new life, he had abruptly thought about his old one.

Then she lifted her glass and stared back at him with one eyebrow raised in that mocking gaze she could do so well.

Jack carefully set his glass down on a nearby table. When the lady said something to her escort and moved away, heading out of the room, Jack hurriedly followed. A quick glance over his shoulder told him that Nan was in the midst of friends and wouldn't notice her groom's absence. He picked up his pace.

He glanced in the side rooms until he came to one that held his prey. She stood on the other side of the room looking out the window. He stepped inside and closed the door after him.

"It can't be," he said huskily, walking swiftly over to her and pulling her into his arms. His mouth covered hers in a heated kiss. "They told me you were dead. There was absolutely no trace of you or any member of the team," he said, punctuating each word with another heated kiss.

She moaned softly under his mouth, then sharply pulled away, turning her back to him.

"Well, Jonathon, this was a surprise," she drawled. "Here I come home, expecting to be welcomed by my husband's open arms. Instead, I learn he has left a perfectly good position to move into another social strata altogether and he has even changed his name. Oh, I forgot another minor change.'' She turned around. "He also got married. There's only one problem with that scenario. He's *still* married.''

Jack could only stare at the woman standing in front of him. He could feel his pulse racing as he just looked at her. He was wrong. She couldn't be his wife! There was so little of the Cassandra he'd seen leave the house more than three years ago. Gone was the mousy brown hair she had always pulled back into a severe twist because she felt it made her look more like a respectable doctor. Now it was heavily streaked with blond highlights and cut in short, feathery wisps around her face. Her normally pale skin was now a deep golden brown, obviously from all that time under the South American sun. Her favorite pearl stud earrings had been replaced with bronze-and-copper disks that dangled against her neck. Her dress was silk and molded to her figure, and she wore high heels that fairly screamed for a man to notice her spectacular legs. But, damn, that mocking arch of the eyebrow was all too familiar! She was the only woman he knew who could do that with such panache.

"What the hell is going on here, Cassandra?'' he demanded, grasping her by the shoulders. "Where have you been? I was told you were dead. Couldn't you have called me before today? When did you get back? *How* did you get back?''

She winced. "Let's not use the *dead* word, shall

we?'' she murmured. She shrugged out of his grasp and explained in a matter-of-fact voice, ''Our guides were murdered by river pirates before we were halfway to our destination. Several of us were wounded and would have died, but some native hunters found us and took us back to their village.'' She straightened up and walked back and forth in the fashion she always used when lecturing in class. ''I fell ill with a fever and had no idea what was going on for close to three months.'' Her features sobered. ''Two of our team died later on.'' She shook her head to clear the disturbing thoughts. She turned to him with a calculating look on her face that made Jack very nervous. ''So tell me, Jonathon. How did you suddenly turn into Jack Larson, living in an exclusive beach town and working for an electronics firm—not to mention marrying the owner's daughter? Do you care to explain *that* to me?''

Jack just stared back at her, clearly at a loss for words. Then his back straightened.

''Considering you've been dead for the past few years, I can safely say that I was within my rights to do whatever I wanted,'' he said tightly. His mind was reeling over seeing her.

''Fine, you're within your rights. But I'm afraid you're going to have to go in there and inform the bride the marriage is off,'' she said huffily. For a moment, he could have sworn he saw uncertainty in her gaze. ''Unless, of course, you'd prefer to stay with

her. If so, you should discard wife number one first.''
She had quickly regained her caustic tongue.

"I'm doing Nan a favor," he said finally before he
decided to wring her lovely neck.

She uttered a sharp laugh. "That's an awfully big
favor to do for a person."

"Dammit, Cassandra!" he growled.

Jack didn't know what to think. He had just gotten
married, but the woman he had married eight years
ago hadn't died, after all. Which meant Nan wasn't
his wife. Except Nan needed a husband right now. As
he thought about it, he saw that Nan needed him now
more than Cassandra had ever needed him. He took
a deep breath.

"Who knows you're back?" he asked.

She frowned. "What does it matter? Oh, all right,"
she huffed. "The military, the institute Greg is affil-
iated with and the team's relatives," she replied. "So
far, it's been kept from the media. We felt it wasn't
that viable a story, anyway, since little had been written about the expedition when we left."

Jack rubbed his forehead. He knew the headache
hammering his temples wasn't from the champagne
he'd drunk but from what he was hearing. How did
this happen?

"This is all too much to take in," he said wearily.

"Pardon me for messing up your life."

Jack was surprised by her sarcasm. Cassandra was
never sarcastic. Biting, yes, but never sarcastic. But

then, he still had trouble believing he was looking at his wife.

He started to say more, but the sound of the door opening caught their attention. The bride, elegant in her cream-colored silk gown, stepped inside. She looked at her groom, then at the stranger with a quizzical smile.

"Darling, people are thinking you've abandoned me before the wedding cake has even been cut." She walked up to Jack and looped her arm through his. She kept an eye on Cassandra.

"Nan, I am so happy to meet you!" Cassandra walked over with a bright smile on her face and her arms outstretched. "I can't believe my nasty ol' brother here could find such a lovely bride."

"Brother?" Nan's tone was perplexed as she warily accepted Cassandra's exuberant hug.

"Are you telling me Jack never mentioned me?" She tsked as she stepped back. "I'm Casey, Jack's baby sister." She favored the groom with a syrupy smile. "I apologize for crashing your wedding, but I just recently found out about it. I've been out of the country for the past few years and just returned not long ago. I'm so glad I got back here in time for your reception."

"I'm sorry, Jack never mentioned he had a sister," Nan said, shooting him a censuring look. "I'm so glad you could come. You're here with a naval officer, aren't you?"

Casey nodded. "A dear friend of the family."

"Dear?" Nan put another connotation to the word.

"No, not that dear." Her laughter tinkled like sparkling water. "Military men tend to think women will fall for the uniform and forget what might be inside it," she confided. "But he makes a more-than-acceptable escort."

Nan laughed along with her. "Come back and meet our friends," she invited as she pulled Jack toward the door. "Are you staying in the area?"

"Actually, I don't have a place to stay," she lied without a qualm. "I'd come for Jack's wedding. To be honest, I was glad to get away from my old place for a while. Very bad memories," she confided with just the right touch.

Jack wasn't sure whether to gag her right then and there or just confess the truth. Casey? She hated that nickname! And to have the nerve to call herself his sister was more than enough to send him spinning. What was she up to? Yes, he needed to explain the situation, but this wasn't the best of times, and he and Nan would be leaving that evening for a luxury condo in Maui for their honeymoon. Honeymoon. He groaned inside. He didn't even want to think about that!

For a man who had lived the stringent academic life, he was suddenly thrown into a mess that would require more than a genius to figure out.

"Then, please stay at our house," Nan invited.

"She can't," he burst out.

Nan looked surprised by his outburst. "Why not? It's not as if we'll be using it for the next two weeks."

"Casey said she's just here for the wedding," he explained, feeling the sweat pouring down his back.

"Thank you, I'd love to stay if you don't mind." She offered a smile that silently asked for reassurance.

"Not at all." Nan gave her the reassurance she needed. "We have a lovely guest house you can stay in."

Once back at the reception, Casey crooked her finger for Ben to come to her. Luckily he picked up on her hint when she made sure to mention Jack as her brother.

Casey silently admitted playing games like this wasn't her style. She was used to using her medical skills and lecturing medical school students once a week. Science was her forte, not acting. But she was a new woman now with a new look and a whole new attitude. Not to mention, she had not only just allowed her husband to marry another woman, but she was allowing him to continue this farce. She admitted she wanted to learn more about what was really going on. While Nan acted like the typical love-struck bride, there was something just a bit stiff about Jack that told her he wasn't acting like the normal groom. The normal groom who sweated through the wedding ceremony, endured the wedding reception and looked forward to the wedding night.

Wedding night? No, that was something she'd rather not think about. She *couldn't* think about the beautiful Nan spending tonight with Jonathon—or Jack. Whoever he was, he was her husband. But as distasteful as his new marriage was, she had to go along with it. At least, until she found out why Jack seemed to want to go on being married to the lovely Nan. Then Casey would charge him with bigamy.

The old Casey didn't believe in practical jokes or getting even. The new Casey did whatever was necessary. She grazed along the buffet table and tried a little bit of everything. When she reached one of the dips, she smiled widely as she piled some on a plate along with crackers and offered it to Jack.

"You'll love this," she cooed, pushing the plate into his hands. "Try some, Jack." She stressed his name.

Smiling, and a little wary, he accepted the plate and tentatively tasted the treat. He smiled. "Nan said the caterer was excellent, and it seems she was right." He quickly ate some more.

Casey kept smiling. If her calculations were right, Jack would figure out her little scheme sometime around bedtime.

"YOU ACTUALLY TOLD HER you were his sister?" Marge giggled. She sat back on the bed, stretching her legs out in front of her.

Casey nodded. She was folding the last of her clothing and placing it in the suitcase. Her tote bag, already packed, sat next to it.

Marge shook her head, unable to take in the story

she had been hearing. "This is so unlike you. I mean, I've heard stories about what a..." Her voice dropped off. She wasn't sure whether her description would insult her new friend.

"What a single-minded, stuffy, boring person I was?" Casey recited without rancor. She sat down on the end of the bed and faced the other woman. "I was that and more," she admitted. "Then I ended up in the middle of the Amazon with no hope of getting back home again. Greg and I were the only survivors, and he had a lot of healing to do before he could get around. The tribespeople didn't speak English, and I had no idea what they were saying. Sign language was helpful, and pretty soon we began to understand one another. Luckily, they didn't view me as some kind of witch for my healing skills, and I didn't look down on them for what I viewed as primitive medical practices." She smiled slightly. "I became a lot more tolerant and open to learning what they were willing to teach me. When we were found, I felt sad at leaving the people who'd taught me how to live again," Casey murmured.

"I can't even imagine what you went through." Marge's gaze was warm with understanding. "Casey, did you ever have a childhood?"

"Not the kind everyone else has. I was too busy with tutors and classes. The perils of your parents discovering you have an extremely high IQ," Casey said wryly. "Playtime didn't teach me anything, so they didn't consider it necessary. The only reason I learned tennis was because it was good for my hand-eye coordination."

"I'm surprised they didn't mind you marrying Jonathon."

"Oh, they did." She laughed. "But I was going through a rebellious phase then. I decided that would be the best way to live my life the way I wanted to." She looked off into the distance as if contemplating a bittersweet memory. "It didn't turn out the way I thought it would. Jonathon was just as rigid in his thoughts as my parents were."

Marge climbed off the bed and paused long enough to pat Casey's shoulder. "Something tells me both of you have changed in the past few years," she said quietly. "Now it's up to you to decide if you want to fight for the man your husband has become or release him to his new life."

Casey looked up. "He's definitely a great deal more challenging than he was three years ago." She recalled Jack, handsome in the tuxedo, and the fleeting look in his eyes when he realized who she was. Her smile was pure female. "But then, I'm not the same woman, either, so it's going to be interesting to see how this all comes out."

Chapter Two

"So this is the newlyweds' cottage," Casey murmured, stopping her car in front of the sprawled-out building. "It's a good thing I have my sunglasses," she said as she viewed the white-on-white house with blue shutters. She guessed the house overlooked the beach, since she could hear the ocean beyond the house. She walked around the rear of her car toward the steps.

"I see you didn't have any problem finding us." Nan stepped outside with a warm smile on her lips. She had changed from her gown into a tailored white silk pantsuit. Her only jewelry was her wedding ring and a pair of diamond stud earrings large enough to blind Casey even with her sunglasses on.

"I thought you would be on your way to your honeymoon hideaway by now," Casey said, surprised by her presence.

Nan shook her head. "Jack and I thought it best to fly out first thing in the morning," she explained. "I had the housekeeper prepare the guest house for you.

That way you'll have some privacy if you wish. Why don't you leave your luggage here? I'll have someone take it over for you." She gestured for Casey to follow her.

The moment Casey stepped inside, she felt as if she was stepping into a sunlit courtyard. She realized the cathedral ceilings and large skylights were the reason. She started at what appeared to be a very large tree in the middle of the living room.

"Do you like our conversation piece?" Nan asked, amused by Casey's reaction. "It seemed a shame to remove the tree, so we just built around it."

"All it needs is a tree house," Casey murmured, following her hostess and covertly glancing around for the groom. Jack couldn't be affected already, could he? What if he didn't have that allergy anymore? She didn't want to think about that. Because, if so, the groom would be consummating a marriage that didn't exist. "I must say this is very generous of you," she went on. "Allowing me to stay here, that is. After all, you're newlyweds, and I would think you would prefer having all the privacy you can have."

"Don't be silly. You're family." She waved off Casey's thanks. "Jack and I are going to be gone, and the guest house would only stand empty, so I don't want you to feel guilty about using it. Stay as long as you like. There's a kitchenette if you prefer to be self-sufficient, but you're more than welcome to eat at the main house. The staff will be here." She led the way through the house and outside onto a large patio.

Casey feared her eyes were saucer-size as she took in the opulence of each room. She had no idea what value beachfront property had nowadays, but she guessed that this house—with the tennis court, a swimming pool, spa and matching guest house—was worth several million. But she couldn't imagine Jack feeling comfortable living here. He was never someone affected by material goods, and this house was beyond anything she had ever seen, so she had to imagine it was new to him, also. Until she remembered he'd had almost three years to grow accustomed to his new life-style while she'd been thrown into hers without any warning.

She took a few covert glances at the upstairs windows. Was Jack up there looking down on them? Speaking of no warning, she laughed to herself, little did Jack know what was in store for him in a few hours.

WHAT WAS SHE TRYING to do? Drive him insane?

Jack stood to the side of the window so he could look down without being seen. He had been surprised that Casey had blithely introduced herself as his sister instead of blurting out the truth in her usual blunt manner as he expected her to do. The only problem was, the Casey he saw and talked to at the reception wasn't the same Cassandra who left for South America three years ago. It wasn't just her chic haircut and bright clothing. It was the way she carried herself, the way she acted.... Dammit, it was everything about her that he couldn't understand!

He stared at Casey, gorgeous in a tangerine T-shirt tucked into shorts that showed a great deal of tanned leg.

"She never used to wear shorts that short and tight," he murmured, still staring at her legs. "Even though she always had the legs for them."

Jack took several deep breaths. Both wives on the same property. The first pretending to be his sister, the second having no idea his sister was his wife. And then there was him right smack in the middle. All he'd done was agree to do a very large favor for the daughter of a man he'd admired these past few years. Little did he realize it would end up in such a complicated situation. And Jack, for all his clear and logical thought processes, had no idea how to untangle what he'd begun.

As he looked out, he idly scratched the back of his hand....

"BY THE TIME the happy couple are thinking about bed this evening, the groom should be experiencing a few nasty symptoms," Casey murmured to herself, glancing at her watch. She finished unpacking and putting away her clothing, then set about to investigate her living quarters. She found the kitchen stocked with the essentials and the refrigerator filled with juices, bottled water and soft drinks. "Self-sufficient is right." She plucked a bottle of water out of the refrigerator and unscrewed the top, drinking as she returned to the bedroom. Giggling, she flopped on the bed and kicked off her shoes. "So this is how the other half lives. I could get used to this."

She had already explained to Nan that she wouldn't join them for dinner, that she preferred to give them some privacy. Nan gave the usual protests, but Casey didn't miss the feigned arguments. Actually, Casey felt it best she remain out of Jack's line of sight for the time being. She didn't want him to instantly think of her when the symptoms flared up.

"I'm a very bad girl," she murmured, lifting the bottle in a toast. "A very bad girl. And I love it!"

"DARLING, ARE YOU FEELING all right?" Nan asked, watching Jack with concern. "You hardly ate a thing at dinner."

"Nerves," he joked, but it fell flat. His nerves had intensified when Nan walked into the room wearing a nightgown that revealed more than it covered. He doubted any man could resist the lovely picture. Even him. The idea that Casey was only yards away made it easy to remain neutral to the war going on inside his body.

She walked over to him and wrapped her arms around his shoulders. "I realize this is all very sudden and you still have feelings for your wife, but—" there was no way she could miss the stiffening in his shoulders. "I appreciate what you're doing for me," Nan murmured, resting her cheek against the top of his head while her hands were busy kneading his shoulders in slow and easy movements that lingered every few seconds. "And I want you to know that I will do everything in my power to make this as pleasurable as possible."

Jack couldn't miss the less-than-subtle scent of Nan's perfume wafting about, the silken feel of her hands on his shoulders and the way her barely covered breasts oh-so-lightly brushed against his back. Jack couldn't believe it—his new wife was seducing him! The new wife who had talked to him about their marriage being in name only, in order for her to keep control of her father's company.

"We're both alone, Jack." Her murmur was husky, breathy in his ear. "Isn't it right that we be together? To keep that lonely feeling at bay? I wonder if it wasn't meant to be?"

With each of Nan's questions, accompanied by the sensual feel of her hands wandering lightly down his chest, came the awareness of something else going on in his body. And it wasn't entirely pleasant.

Jack wasn't even aware he was busily scratching the back of his hand and up his arm until he accidentally scratched Nan.

"Jack!" She drew back quickly. She leaned over his shoulder and stared down at his arms. "What have you done to yourself?"

The shock in her voice was enough to make him look down. Nasty red blotches covered both arms. He opened his shirt and found the same blossoms across his chest. It seemed just staring at it started the itching full force. He uttered a curse under his breath.

You'll love this. Try some, Jack.

The plate with the pink-colored dip. He'd had more than one helping because he'd found the dip so tasty and he'd been too nervous to eat earlier in the day.

"Oh, darling! I'm calling the doctor." Nan hurried to the phone.

"No." He gritted against the itching that made its nasty way across his entire body. "Just get my sister." He practically snarled the last word.

"Your sister?" She picked up the receiver. "What can she do?"

"She's a doctor. She'll know what to do." *Oh, yes, she knows exactly what to do.*

"She is? She never mentioned it." Nan pulled an equally unsubstantial robe over her nightgown. "I'll go down and get her." Her forehead wrinkled slightly as she watched him furiously scratch his chest. "I'll be back as soon as soon as possible, sweetheart."

Jack slouched down in his chair, pulling his shirt open and furiously scratching his chest. He knew from past experience that scratching only made it worse, but the knowledge of how he got into this miserable state only made him scratch more.

"I DON'T UNDERSTAND what happened," Nan cried, after hurriedly explaining her presence.

"It sounds as if he had an allergic reaction to something," Casey said in her professional voice. She picked up a black leather satchel and followed Nan out of the guest house. "Jack does have some food allergies. What did he have for dinner?"

"We had roast lamb and a lemon soufflé for dessert." She looked worried. "Do you think we should call an ambulance? I've heard of people dying from allergic reactions."

"Let me take a look at him first." The corners of Casey's lips twitched. She didn't have to look at Jack to know it wasn't deadly, but he would be very uncomfortable for a few days. A serious expression overtook her face when Nan looked over her shoulder as they walked up the stairs.

Nan grimaced prettily as she stopped in front of a closed door. "I'm very sorry, but I'm not very good around sick people," she murmured her apology. "I either hover too much or if there's blood..." She turned pale.

"Don't worry about it," Casey assured her, placing her hand on the other woman's arm. "A lot of people have trouble with illness. It's nothing to be ashamed of. I'll go in and examine Jack. Why don't you go downstairs and try to relax. I'll be down as soon as possible to give you my diagnosis."

As she opened the door she noticed Nan slowly walking down the hallway.

"Well, brother dear, what have you done to yourself?" she asked Jack as she stepped inside and closed the door behind her.

By now, he was wild-eyed. "*Me?* Why don't you tell me what *you* did to me?" he demanded between clenched teeth.

"Stop that." Casey slapped his hands away from his chest. She studied the angry red blotches with a professional veneer. "I may be wrong, but I'd say you had an allergic reaction. You haven't been walking through poison ivy or poison oak, have you? No, I guess not." She tapped her chin with her forefinger. "Now, if I remember correctly, you're allergic to penicillin. But, frankly, I didn't see that at the wedding reception." She opened her bag and rummaged through the contents. She finally held up a vial and a wrapped disposable syringe. "This injection should help the itching, but you've got a pretty good case, so I'll have to give you more than usual."

Jack winced as he watched the needle plunge through the rubber stopper. His eyes couldn't leave the sight of the torturous device as Casey held it up. She made sure the dosage was correct, then tapped the barrel to dispel any air bubbles. Shots of any kind were not one of his favorite activities. Yet, the view in front of him helped a great deal.

He couldn't remember seeing any doctor wearing what Casey wore at that moment. To be honest, he couldn't remember Casey ever wearing anything so revealing.

Her gauzy tank top bared a few inches of her flat midriff, while the wide waistband of her flowing, ankle-length skirt was decorated by a three-strand gold chain belt. Her feet were bare, with coral-tipped toes peeking out from under the fabric of her skirt. The same coral shade glossed her lips. He couldn't remember her ever wearing lipstick. And certainly nothing like the smoky shadow on her lids that gave her eyes a mysterious cast.

He was so engrossed in the pure female picture standing before him he didn't immediately react when she expertly turned him over and pulled down his pajama bottoms. He yelped when the cold alcohol swab hit his skin, and he yelped even louder when she administered the injection.

"Why the hell did you do that?" he demanded, rolling over.

"See, fast, no fuss, no muss. If I'd told you to pull down your pants, you would have argued that you didn't think your baby sister should see your cute butt." Casey smiled as she put everything away in the case. "This way, you didn't have to worry about any protests."

"Isn't it amazing you had everything right on hand," Jack muttered darkly.

"That's what a doctor is for," she said brightly. "Just like a Boy Scout. Be prepared."

He eyed her narrowly.

"Where's Nan?" he demanded.

"Downstairs. She apologized, explaining she isn't very good in a sickroom." Casey perched herself on the footstool in front of Jack. "The medication should be kicking in soon."

He still glared at her. "What did you give me?"

She looked wide-eyed, all innocence in her gaze. "I'm sure I don't know what you mean. I gave you an anti-inflammatory to relieve the itching."

"I mean the dip." Now that the itching was starting to subside, his anger was taking over with a vengeance.

"It was very good, wasn't it? I'll have to tell Nan." She rested her elbow on her knee, her chin propped up on her cupped hand.

"What kind was it?"

She wasn't the least bit fazed by his fury. "Crab dip." She lifted her head, looking surprised, as if a thought just occurred to her. "Wait a minute. That's it! The crab dip! Oh, Jack, I completely forgot. You're allergic to shellfish." She pursed her lips in concern. "You poor baby. No wonder you're suffering so much."

"You never forget anything," Jack stated between teeth clenched so tightly his jaw ached. "You don't have a brain. You have a computer in your head. You did this deliberately."

She crossed her arms in front of her chest, her flat palms against her collarbone as she looked the picture of injured innocence.

"I am shocked you would think that of me. Although, you have to admit it would have been a little sticky if you had consummated your marriage to Nan while you're still married to me. Oh, I understand you thought I was dead. But as you can see, I'm very much alive. And, as we both know, society frowns on a man having two wives."

"We hadn't planned on consummating the marriage," he told her in a modified roar.

That statement brought surprise to her face. She sat up straighter as she absorbed his words. "What do you mean you weren't going to consummate it?"

How he hated even talking about this. "Simple. Nan needed a husband to keep control of her father's company. She knew my wife was dead and hoped I'd be willing to help her out. We'd remain married for about two years, then have a quiet divorce."

"Have you and Nan been dating for some time?"

He shook his head. "Not really. Oh, we'd have dinner sometimes or attend social functions together. But there wasn't any romance between us."

Casey looked doubtful. "Nan is a beautiful woman. I would think she could have her pick of men."

"Meaning, why me?" His mouth twisted. "Her father almost died from a heart attack. He felt it was time to retire and he wanted to know his company and his daughter were well taken care of. I guess she's made a few wrong choices in the past. Norton doesn't realize that Nan is more than capable of taking care of herself, so to help her out, I told him I'd marry her. It eased his mind and helped his recovery."

"And he considered you suitable," she said quietly.

He nodded.

"And what do you get out of it?"

That was something Jack preferred not to discuss. "That has nothing to do with this."

She inclined her head. "What does she know about me?"

He shifted uncomfortably under her direct gaze. "Very little. I told her my wife was on a scientific expedition in another country when she died."

Casey looked as if she wasn't sure she appreciated the brevity of his statement. Even if it did make it easier for her to masquerade as his sister.

"Except..."

She couldn't miss his uneasy manner or the fact he refused to look at her. One thing Jack had never been able to do was lie to her.

"Except what?" she asked sharply.

He took a deep breath. He was afraid she might regret giving him the medication.

"Nan started talking about how there was no reason we couldn't make this a real marriage," he said finally.

Casey slowly stood up. Her skirt floated around her ankles. "I think I've heard enough for one evening," she said quietly. "I also know that the medication I gave you used to make you pretty sleepy, so I'll leave you to sleep it off."

Jack could feel weariness steal into his bones and his eyelids growing heavy.

"Why did you have to come back now?" His words were slurred, and his eyelids were closing, so he didn't see the pain cross her face.

"Sweet dreams, Jonathon," she whispered as she slipped out of the room.

As Casey walked down the stairs, she could hear Nan talking softly to someone.

"I don't know what happened. He was covered with horrible red blotches and he was scratching like a dog with a bad case of fleas," she murmured.

As Casey rounded a corner and looked into the great room she could see Nan standing in front of a bow window. She held a cordless phone to her ear as she paced back and forth.

"I must go. I'll talk to you later. Yes, I do," she whispered before pressing the disconnect button. She looked up, noting Casey's presence. "I'm sorry. I didn't know you were finished. How is he?"

Casey wasn't sure, but she thought a look of guilt crossed Nan's beautiful features.

"I'm afraid he's knocked out for the night," she replied, coming in and sitting down in a nearby chair. "It was a food allergy. He said he had some of that crab dip. He had no idea what it was, and with his allergy to shellfish it was natural he'd break out. I'm sorry your wedding night was ruined."

Nan picked up a bottle of wine and filled two glasses. She handed one to Casey.

"I'm just relieved he's all right." She sat in the chair across from her as she sipped her wine. "I'm afraid I don't know anything about you. Jack hasn't talked about his family very much."

"That's all right. I don't know about you, either,"

Casey admitted. She tasted the wine. "Jack and I haven't been in much contact the past few years." She knew keeping her story simple was the only way not to trip herself up.

"Was there a reason for the two of you not to remain in contact?" Nan asked delicately.

She paused, trying to formulate a reply that would sound plausible. "I've been doing a lot of traveling overseas the past few years, and since I wasn't always sure where I'd be, it was difficult to keep in touch. I enjoyed the chance to learn new medical treatments." She smiled to herself, thinking of some of the treatments she had learned that would be considered unorthodox at the very least. Not to mention so many other things she had learned about people in general, and herself, as she lived in primitive conditions.

"Then, I hope we'll have the chance to get to know each other better." Nan smiled as she lifted her glass up in a toast.

Casey did the same. "I would like that. I feel as if we'll discover we have a great deal in common."

Chapter Three

Jack was in the midst of a slow and ugly death. Once he died he knew he'd make a very disgusting-looking corpse. He'd never had a hangover in his life, but this had to be one. Nothing else could make him feel this ill.

Then he remembered the insane events of the previous day. Correction. There was something that could pump even more acid into his stomach. That something was Cassandra. No, Casey now. Cassandra was always winter-pale with serene features and never raised her voice. She wore sensible clothing and never did anything without considering the ramifications.

Casey had deep gold skin and laughing features that had more than a hint of sensuality in them. Her clothing was colorful and showed off a lovely body. She freely spoke her mind and obviously didn't think before leaping.

The night before, even as his body screamed for a horizontal position, he forced himself out of bed and staggered over to the window when he heard Casey leave the house. He couldn't understand why she stayed for more than an hour after leaving him. What had she and Nan talked about during that time? His mind refused to consider what went on. The lights dotting the path between the house and guest house highlighted her figure, making her look like a ghostly entity walking the stone pathway. The evening breeze swept under her skirt, making it fly up against her, baring her legs and thighs. He imagined her laughter as she tried to push it back down, then finally gave up and allowed it to fly around her.

Jack thought of the times they had made love. Perhaps it wasn't the right subject to think of on his wedding night, but seeing Casey brought back memories of their wedding night. Casey had been a virgin who admitted to being well versed in the mechanics of lovemaking but had no personal experience. Jack had lost his virginity at seventeen when his hormones had been running wild, but he hadn't considered the act all that exciting. But with Casey it had been special. Warm and comforting. Perhaps they hadn't seen fireworks, but they hadn't minded because they simply enjoyed each other.

She had never worn a revealing nightgown like the one Nan had on tonight. And she had never taken the initiative. Now he wondered how he was going to tell Nan their marriage wasn't valid when the woman obviously had other ideas.

He had gone to bed, feeling very unfaithful to two women. He was unfaithful to Casey for marrying another woman and unfaithful to Nan for thinking about Casey. His sleep had been marred by disjointed dreams, and he awoke feeling more dead than alive.

He closed his eyes against the elves pounding away inside his head. Then he realized some of the pounding was someone tapping at the door.

"Jack, may I come in?" Nan called out.

"Yes, please." He wondered if his usual early morning scruffiness would scare her.

Nan stepped inside, carrying a tray. Her smile dimmed a bit when she looked at him, unshaven and obviously unkempt.

"I thought you deserved breakfast in bed," she told him as she set the tray down on a table by the window. "How are you feeling?"

He looked down at his bare arms. "The blotches have pretty well cleared up and the itching has subsided."

"Then it sounds as if you're going to live, after all," she said gaily. She poured him coffee and handed him a cup. She filled a second for himself.

Jack stared at the plate filled with an omelette and hash brown potatoes. Various Danish pastries filled a napkin-lined basket and a glass of orange juice finished the meal.

"There's enough here for both of us."

"Oh, I've already eaten. I asked Casey over for an early breakfast." She sipped her coffee.

"Nonsense, you can eat one of these." He put a croissant on a plate and handed it to her.

Nan broke off a piece of the flaky confection and carried it to her lips.

"Your sister is a lovely person," she said. "We had a wonderful talk last night and again this morning."

Jack could feel his stomach tighten into the size of a pea. "Oh?" It took all of his self-control to chew a mouthful of omelette.

"She's very well traveled and so passionate about medicine. She talked about some of the alternative methods she's learned the past few years and how she feels some of them are much better than anything modern medicine has to offer. I asked her if she plans to open a practice in the area, but she said she hadn't given it any thought. I suggested she think about it now."

Jack tried his coffee. Good, it was hot and strong. He needed the caffeine to clear his head.

"Casey has always preferred teaching to practicing," he murmured.

"Yes, she did mention she'd lectured premed students, but she's since discovered she enjoys helping people," Nan replied. "I had no idea your sister is a true genius." She shook her head in amazement. "Can you imagine attending high school when your age is more suited for grammar school? How did the rest of your family handle having a genius in their midst? And you. It must have been difficult for you even with your above-average intelligence."

"I let her do my homework," Jack muttered, for lack of anything better to say.

Judging by Nan's amusement, she believed him. She tore off another bit of croissant and nibbled on it. She stared out the window for a moment before turning back to him.

"I was wondering, darling. What with your illness last night and all, perhaps we should postpone our honeymoon for a little while," she said. "We could do some traveling later in the year."

"When you feel your position is more solid with the firm?" he asked, with a hint of teasing in his tone.

Nan wrinkled her nose and laughed. "You know me too well."

Jack looked at Nan and wondered why he had never felt truly attracted to her. She was beautiful, intelligent, had a wonderful sense of humor and was one of the kindest women he'd ever met. She had so much to offer. In some ways, more than Casey ever had. But then Casey was the first to admit she was limited in some areas due to her restricted upbringing. At least Nan had had a childhood, even if it had been a vastly privileged one. And she was not the least bit a spoiled socialite who thought of nothing but shopping and hair appointments. She enjoyed the intensity of the business world and had a keen mind for negotiations. He only wished her father would see the prize he had in his daughter instead of slighting her with menial tasks and using her as his hostess for business functions.

Norton had felt the corporation should be run under a man and had gone so far as to marry off his daughter to someone he approved of. Otherwise, he had threatened the company would be run by the board of directors, who would choose their own head. When Nan had approached Jack with her idea of their marrying, he had rejected the idea at first. He had made his rejection as gentle as possible, explaining that he hadn't planned to marry again. Not to mention, he was still accustoming himself to a nonacademic lifestyle. Nan had easily pushed aside all his objections with the explanation the marriage would be in name only and only for as long as it took her to show her father she knew what she was doing. Then they could divorce quietly, and she would help him in any way he wished with a settlement. Jack had no wish for cash, but he found appealing the idea of doing something truly useful, especially since it was to help out his friend and mentor, Norton Xavier.

What he hadn't counted on was the wife he'd been told was dead coming back. Except she wasn't the same woman who'd left three years ago. Not in looks and, even more, not in personality. What had happened to her down there to effect all these changes? He vowed to have a good long talk with her as soon as possible. He'd feel a hell of a lot better if he knew exactly what was going on.

"Are you still feeling bad?" Nan asked, interrupting his train of thought.

He looked up, then realized he hadn't eaten a bite

for several minutes. "I'm feeling a lot better. If I'd known that was crab dip, I would have made sure to stay as far away as possible."

"I'm just glad your sister was here to take care of you." Nan reached across and patted the back of his head.

"Yes, it was fortunate," Jack said darkly. "Where is she now?"

"She wanted to take a walk on the beach."

"She hates the beach!"

Nan jumped at his vehement tone.

"What I mean is, should she go down there alone?" He silently cursed himself for overreacting.

"You know very well the beach is private, other than the Pattersons, and they'll be in Jamaica for another month," she replied.

"I'm sorry, Nan. This isn't exactly the way I'd visualized our honeymoon," he muttered.

"That's all right. We have plenty of time for one," she assured him as she rose to her feet. "If you don't mind, I think I'll make some calls. I already let the Shepherds know we won't be joining them for dinner tomorrow evening." She mentioned the couple they'd planned to see while on their honeymoon.

Jack nodded. That was fine with him. Bill Shepherd couldn't seem to talk about anything but stock futures, and Lilith, his wife, was only concerned with redecorating their house every year. Last he'd heard, she was considering redesigning in an Egyptian motif.

The idea of dining with a sarcophagus looking over his shoulder was more than any man could bear.

"I think I'll go down and check on Casey," he said.

"Don't do anything strenuous," she advised on her way out. "After all, you were very ill last night."

"Yes, and I know the reason why," he muttered grimly, tackling the rest of his breakfast.

CASEY HAD WALKED ALONG the waterline until she was in front of the neighboring house, then she turned around and leisurely walked back to Nan and Jack's house.

"Amazing. I've only been considered dead less than three years and he's already replaced me," she groused, kicking the sand with her bare feet. "If I'd heard he'd been killed in the Amazon, I wouldn't have replaced him for at least five years. Maybe even ten." She turned around and faced the water. For many, the gently rolling waves would have been soothing. For Casey, right now, nothing was soothing.

She hoped she had given Jack enough medication to keep him sleeping for a while. The idea that last night was his wedding night didn't set well with her. As far as she was concerned, he could sleep for the next year.

"I would have given him a lovely funeral, too. Complete with noisemakers and party hats," she muttered, kicking the sand even harder. Except this time, her bare toes encountered something hard enough to send pain shooting up her leg. "Damn!" She hopped on one foot then dropped to the sand to cradle her injured foot.

"Serves you right for making fun of my funeral," Jack told her, dropping down in front of her and taking her foot into his hands. He gently rotated it from side to side. The toes were a bright red but not bleeding.

"I kicked a rock," she muttered, jerking her foot out of his hands. She scooted back and sat cross-legged on the sand. "I thought you'd still be asleep."

"Obviously, you didn't give me enough to knock me out for more than ten hours," Jack told her, likewise sitting back.

Casey looked at him, noticing the lightweight navy shorts and faded yellow T-shirt he wore. She suddenly looked serious. "What happened to you while I was gone? You're not the same."

"I needed to make some changes in my life. I was lucky enough to meet Norton, and he helped me discover just what was out there. I owe a lot to him bringing me back to reality," he said quietly. "What about you? You're not exactly the same, either."

"I decided it was time to start living instead of stagnating," she said simply. "When you realize you could have died a horrible death, you discover another part of yourself that tells you it might be a good time to find out just why life is worth living. It's even easier to do when you live with a tribe that takes life as a day-by-day celebration." She leaned forward, her face alight with the intensity that seemed to drive her.

"These people would be called primitive barbarians by our society. No running water, no electricity, no modern facilities at all and no medical care other than their medicine man who handled all the ills of the tribe. Some of the potions and poultices he used would look ridiculous in our eyes, and while some weren't effective, others were." She used her hands for emphasis as she spoke. "There was a little boy who couldn't have been more than four years old. He had a horrible fever. We had been lucky to have salvaged most of our medical supplies, but the parents refused to allow us to treat him. I, in my God-complex as a doctor, said the boy didn't have to die. They believed their medicine man could help him. The medicine man wasn't too happy about a woman interfering, and he proceeded to show me just what skills I lacked." Her voice dropped to a softer level. "He told me my medicine was not favored by their gods. That it would only have made the little boy worse. I refused to believe him, but later on, I came to realize if I'd followed the prescribed treatment for the boy, he would have died."

"Why? Because the gods didn't like you?"

Casey shook her head at his sarcasm. "Because I was looking at treating the fever, not at what caused it. I was very lucky. Their medicine man could have ordered the villagers to kill me, but he didn't. He said

I needed to listen to the gods of the jungle and learn what plants heal and what plants kill."

Jack looked as if he couldn't believe what he was hearing. "You always scorned alternative medicine. You said it was something that should have been left in the sixties and that it had no place in modern medicine."

"And I was wrong," she said simply. "During that time, the medicine man and I taught each other things."

"I can imagine what you taught him," he murmured.

"I taught him that washing his hands before examining a wound is a good idea, and that what they used as beer also made an excellent disinfectant," she said smugly.

"Isn't that nice? You and the local doctor shared medical secrets while family and friends thought you were dead." His words cut her like glass.

Casey was surprised steam wasn't coming out of Jack's ears as he glared at her.

"We had no idea where we were," she argued. "It took Greg months to recover, and by then I was resigned to the fact we'd live out the rest of our lives with the tribe. Our radio equipment had been destroyed. Needless to say, neither Greg nor I had any knowledge of how to fix it."

Jack mentally recalled the good-looking scientist who had picked Casey up that last day. "And what did Greg do while you played jungle doctor?"

She grimaced. "He was slower to come around to their way of thinking. Although he didn't seem to mind the idea the women wore only a piece of cloth around their hips."

Jack stared out at the ocean. He was sorely tempted to ask Casey if she had indulged in the custom, but he wasn't sure he wanted to know. So far, though, he hadn't seen any tan lines.

"So tell me, Jack. How did you sleep last night?" she asked.

Talk about the perfect way to get his mind off her walking around the jungle half naked.

"You sabotaged my wedding night."

She considered his accusation. "No, I made sure you didn't compound your crime of bigamy. You should be thankful I was able to save you. Especially—" her voice hardened "—since you preferred to remain married to her instead of telling her the truth."

"I told you why," he said between clenched teeth. "Nan is the one who should be running her father's company, but he refuses to admit she has the intelligence to do it. He's still of the old school that women should be hostesses and mothers."

Casey shook her head. "That's a very archaic reasoning. Why didn't she just prove to him she could do it, and he would have handed it over to her when he retired?"

"He had a heart attack and thought he'd die. He

asked me to marry Nan and make sure the company went on as before."

She arched an eyebrow. "And being a good Boy Scout, you agreed to it."

"I thought you were dead!"

"Except I'm not."

"I know that." He took a deep breath. How could he explain this? Lecturing had been so much easier. It was even more difficult when his audience was his wife with that dangerously high IQ and a very analytical mind. "Nan's dream has always been to take over for her father. She excelled at Harvard Business School, and her father still refused to see her as executive material. She had to fight her way into the company, and she's worked hard to maintain her standing there." He picked up a handful of sand and allowed it to stream out of his closed fist. "I have to admire her for being willing to take anything thrown at her. It was just a shame her father hasn't bothered to see her abilities. He should have allowed her to gradually take charge over the past few years and take some of the pressure off him. He might have been able to avoid the heart attack," he murmured.

Casey could hear the sorrow in Jack's voice and guessed he greatly admired Nan's father.

"What you're saying is he saw you as the son he didn't have. A philosophy professor," she drawled. "My, my, amazing you could move in the big business circles so swiftly. I've always thought of that kind of pool filled with sharks and barracudas. How did a minnow manage to handle all those predators?''

Jack stood up so quickly he almost lost his balance in the soft sand.

''Even with all the changes in your outward appearance, it's apparent you haven't changed one bit. You're still the coldhearted bitch you were when you left.'' He walked off as swiftly as he could.

She should have turned to stone under his ferocity. Casey looked over her shoulder, watching him head for the stairs. He never looked back during his climb.

If he had, he would have seen the sheen in her eyes and the pain etched on her face. Not that she felt his accusations were untrue. What hurt was the fact that what he'd said *was* true.

JACK ABSENTLY NOTICED Nan was on the phone as he passed her office. He headed for the kitchen and immediately poured himself a cup of coffee. He only hoped the caffeine would help clear his head. He stood by the curved space of windows in the breakfast nook, where he had an unobstructed view of the stairs that led to the beach. The clock told him it was more than twenty minutes before Casey appeared at the top of the stairs. He watched her walk in the direction of the guest house and disappear inside.

Damn! He could feel the muscles inside his body tighten until he thought they would snap with the tension he couldn't ignore.

For a man who'd always lived a pretty uncomplicated life, he had no idea what to do when that quiet life was suddenly turned upside down. Admittedly, he knew his marriage to Nan was going to make some radical changes, but they were minuscule compared to what was going on now that Casey was here. How was he supposed to handle himself in front of Nan while pretending Casey was his sister?

Acid filled his stomach as a brief memory of the night before invaded his mind. Nan and her revealing negligee... Nan and her delicate fingers trailing over his shoulders... Nan and her breasts pressed against his back... This was far from a woman who'd intended a marriage in name only. Oh, God, he thought. He was in trouble. Big trouble. He knew there was just one thing he could do—but how was he going to manage to stay away from his wife? She wanted him to make love to her!

"There you are."

At the mere sound of Nan's voice, Jack jumped. Hurriedly he set the coffee cup down before he dropped it.

Nan walked over to the coffeemaker and filled a cup for herself. "How are you feeling?"

"Much better. The fresh air seemed to help," he muttered, picking his cup up again. He needed to hold on to something.

"I always did enjoy this view." She walked over to stand next to him. She tilted her head so she could look at him easier. "Please don't take this the wrong way...." He silently inclined his head for her to continue. "But could last night have also been a bit of nerves? After all, you hadn't expected to remarry, and all of this did happen suddenly."

Jack would have preferred not meeting her eyes as he answered her, but hell, he was an adult, he had to.

"It's true I hadn't expected to remarry," he said slowly. "But you knew that from the beginning. I know I probably sound like a nervous bride, but I did explain to you that I still have very strong feelings for my wife."

"Of course you would, what with the tragic way you lost her." Her hand rested on his shoulder. Her fingers pressed gently against his shirt as she stood by him. "I understand that, and I'm very grateful to you for helping me out." Her lips brushed against his ear. "I just want you to know you won't regret going through with this."

Jack couldn't help but inhale the rich scent of her perfume. For a man who didn't consider himself imaginative, he could visualize fingers fashioned of silvery smoke stroking his neck and shoulders in a tantalizing fashion. Not good, not good at all.

It had been a long time for him, and Nan's femininity was setting off some loud and clear signals in his brain.

"You know, seducing you could be very enjoyable," she continued to whisper as her fingers traveled down his arm.

Jack took a deep breath—and a chance.

"Why, Mrs. Larson, are you courting me?" he

asked in a playful tone, sending her a look that he hoped looked just as playful.

Nan's lips curved in a smile that was more seductive than fun-loving. "The wife courting the husband. How delicious." She turned away and took a sip of her coffee. "True, we didn't exactly have a normal courtship, did we?" Her smile still curved her lips. "I think that's a wonderful idea." She looked up when something outside the window caught her attention. "Are you and your sister very close?"

"Closer than we were as children," he said smoothly. For a man accustomed to telling the truth, he was turning into a habitual liar. He knew if he was Pinocchio his nose would be a good six feet long by now. "I hope you don't mind her staying here."

"Not at all. In fact, I'll make a point of taking her to the club with me one day. I can introduce her to people there. I'm sure some of the men there would be delighted to keep her company while she's here." She suddenly flashed him a look filled with mischief. "Wouldn't it be lovely if she met someone and decided to settle down around here?"

Jack could feel the noose tightening even more around his neck. He was beginning to hate this whole farce. He was even ready to confess the entire story to Nan. He couldn't have two wives! It was illegal and immoral. And it was unfair to Casey. Even if he had married Nan in good conscience with the knowledge that Casey was dead. How did he know she'd show up again? Or that the Casey who came back to him was infinitely more appealing than the one who'd left? And was it fair for Nan to lose her dream? She had discussed her plan for the company's future and it looked good. Could he deny her her dream after all her father had done for him?

He was beginning to wish he was the one who had gone down to the Amazon. It would have been much easier that way, and he wouldn't be in this damned situation right now.

Before he could break down and damn the consequences and confess all, the door chimes echoed through the house.

"Who can that be?" Nan murmured, setting down her cup. "Louise is at the store, so I'll see who's there." She walked off.

Jack stayed where he was, listening to the clicking of Nan's heels on the tile floor, then the front door opening. Nan's voice sounded surprised then subdued as she greeted the visitor. When he heard the muted tones of a man's voice, Jack decided to go see for himself.

"You can't be here now!" He could hear Nan's low-voiced fury as he walked down the hall.

"Is there a problem, honey?" Jack asked, walking up to her and settling a possessive arm around her shoulders. He wasn't sure, but he sensed Nan wasn't happy to see the man standing in the doorway.

"Darling, this is my cousin, Dan," she said a shade too brightly. "He just moved out to California and stopped by."

"Sorry I couldn't be here yesterday for your wedding," Dan said, holding his hand out to Jack.

Jack couldn't miss the dark tan of a man who spent most of his time outdoors and the easy way he wore casual clothes that cost a small fortune.

"More company?"

Nan and Jack looked out to where Casey was climbing the front steps.

"My cousin has come for a visit," Nan explained. "Casey, my cousin, Dan Reynolds. Dan, this is Jack's sister, Casey, who's also here for a visit."

"My, my," Dan murmured, taking Casey's hand in his. "It seems I came just at the right time."

Casey looked past Dan toward Jack and smiled brightly. "How nice. A family affair."

Chapter Four

"What brought you out this way?" Casey asked in a friendly voice as she settled in a marine-blue-and-white-print cushioned chair that overlooked the swimming pool.

She had taken over immediately, suggesting they adjourn to the rear patio for coffee. Nan murmured something about making a fresh pot and disappeared in the direction of the kitchen. Jack followed Casey and Dan to the patio.

"The company I was with downsized and I was one of the victims," Dan explained, taking the chair next to Casey's. "I thought I'd take a chance on coming out this way and see what I could get into."

Casey nodded her understanding. "And what do you do?"

"I'm a computer analyst." He smiled.

Jack just sat there and seethed. He already decided he didn't like good ol' cousin Dan with his hundred-watt smile, movie star good looks and graceful way of lounging in a chair.

"Which side of the family do you come from?" Casey asked, smiling back at Dan with all the brilliance of a star in the galaxy.

"My mother's sister is his mother," Nan said as she walked out, carrying a large tray. Jack and Dan both hopped up immediately to help her. Jack won by a fraction of a second. He took the tray from her and set it on the table. Nan took the remaining chair and poured four cups of coffee, dispensing them with the grace of a born hostess. She smiled at Dan. "Aunt Jessica moved back east not long after she married. My mother and I used to fly back to see her every fall. As for Dan, I can only say he was a severe trial for me and his sister. He always thought it was his goal in life to make our lives miserable. How is Janice, by the way?"

"Still looking for Mr. Right," he said breezily. "She's jealous that you were so lucky."

Since their chairs were fairly close together, Nan was able to reach over to thread her fingers through Jack's.

"Daddy said he feels that now I'm taken care of he can retire and consider that around-the-world cruise he's always wanted to take," Nan said. "I can't imagine him ever retiring. He loves the company too much."

From Casey's angle, she could see a telling look pass between Nan and Dan. Nan and Dan. She inwardly groaned. Their names together sounded much too cute. She would have to be careful and try not to say or think their names at the same time again or she might erupt into hysterical giggles.

"What about you, Casey?" Dan turned the tables. "What do you do?"

"Isn't that getting a little personal?" Jack asked testily.

"I don't mind. After all, he was open with me," she said airily, waving her hand in the air. "I'm a doctor."

"Medical or Ph.D.?"

"Medical."

Dan nodded. "What specialty?"

"I prefer general practice," she replied. "But I've been traveling a great deal for the past few years, so I haven't been practicing actively."

"I told her she should try to find something around here," Nan chimed in. "I'm sure Daddy could introduce her to some people who could help her."

Casey smiled her thanks at her "sister-in-law" but inwardly thought about throwing up. The last thing she wanted to do was accept any kind of assistance from Nan or her father. Still, a cynical part whispered, she'd lent them her husband, why shouldn't she accept some help from them?

"I think I'll wait a little while before I dive back into my work," she explained.

"I'm surprised the two of you aren't off on your honeymoon," Dan spoke up.

"Poor Jack had a horrible allergic reaction to some food last night." Nan smiled and squeezed Jack's hand. "We thought we'd wait before taking off by ourselves. And now, with the two of you here, we couldn't just abandon you."

"But you should be on your honeymoon," Casey said in an airy voice. "I'm sure Dan can take care of himself." She turned to smile at the other man.

"I'm sure I'd be fine. Especially with Jack's lovely sister here." He returned her smile.

Casey couldn't help but notice the brief glare Jack divided between her and Dan. And she wasn't too surprised to notice Nan looked a little uncomfortable with Dan's blatant attempt at flirting.

"Be careful, Dan," Nan warned with a light laugh. "Some people might take you seriously. Poor Casey just got out of an ugly relationship, so I don't think she's looking for a new attraction just now."

"Oh, I don't know," Casey drawled, lazily stretching her arms over her head. Her top rose up a few inches, revealing a flat, tanned midriff. Two pairs of men's eyes were instantly riveted on the sight. One pair held blatant male interest; the other looked not too happy about the enticing sight.

Casey first favored Dan with a blazing smile that obviously set the man back on his heels, then she turned to Nan. "Don't worry, Nan, I promise to be gentle with your cousin."

"Mom wouldn't like to hear anything like that," Jack grumbled.

"Oh, please, Mom taught me everything I know." Casey turned to Nan. "He does so love playing the role of the protective big brother. But I've reminded him I'm an adult now. And if he wants me to stay out of his love life, he'll have to stay out of mine.'' She batted her eyelashes in a mock flirtatious manner at Jack. ''Big brothers tend to be overbearing at times.''

Jack coughed and looked away.

Casey's smile widened. Good, she'd hit a nerve. If he felt he had to act the part of another woman's husband, he'd have to get used to seeing his wife spread her wings. She may have spent the first thirty years of her life as a drab little moth, but she had quickly learned that living as a butterfly was proving to be much more fun. It hadn't taken her long to realize there was another side to her personality, a side that wanted to play instead of work.

''Oh, dear, now who could that be?'' Nan murmured, lifting her head at the sound of the telephone ringing. With an apologetic smile, she rose from her chair and walked toward the house.

''You were lucky to find Nan and Jack here, Dan,'' Casey said conversationally. ''As you know, Jack was very ill last night.''

Dan's gaze swung in Jack's direction. ''And here I thought it was the bride who got bridal jitters,'' he joked.

Jack's thin-lipped smile held no humor and no explanation.

''Food allergies can be very nasty,'' Casey murmured, shifting to cross her legs, drawing both men's gaze's to her bare legs. "Jack was actually lucky it wasn't worse."

"Really? I've never had any health problems," Dan said archly, looking in Casey's direction. "Care to give me a physical, Doc?"

She was in the midst of thinking of an appropriate reply when Nan walked out of the house. There was no missing the disturbed expression marring her features.

"That was my father," she said in a voice that was a bit higher-pitched than usual. "Since we didn't go to Hawaii, he'd like us to come over for dinner this evening." Her smile seemed strained as she turned to Casey and Dan. "The two of you are also invited."

Jack frowned. "Are you sure this is a good idea?" he asked in a low voice.

"You know Daddy," Nan whispered back. "It's never a request but a command."

Dan looked from one to the other. "Is there a problem?"

"Honeymooners don't exactly expect to have dinner with Dad," Jack said.

"They don't expect to share living space with relatives, either," Casey piped up. "Nan, please thank your father for the kind invitation, but I think I'll have to decline for this evening."

Nan grimaced. "He really wants to meet you, Casey. He's very strong-minded when it comes to family and he'll expect you to be there." She smiled her apology for her father's high-handed manner.

Casey shrugged, gracefully giving in. "You must be happy to see your uncle again, Dan," she commented.

"I haven't seen Uncle Norton in years," Dan said easily.

Casey stood up. "Well, I think I'm going to go into town and do some window-shopping. What time should I be ready?"

"At six," Nan replied.

"I'll be back in time."

As she walked off, she listened to the conversation behind her.

"If Dan's her cousin, I'm Jack's sister," she muttered to herself. She suddenly stopped and a smile lit her face. "But I don't think I'll let Jack in on my suspicions just yet."

"I THOUGHT NORTON WAS TOO ill for strenuous activities," Jack said to Nan later that afternoon.

"Daddy isn't supposed to do anything that can affect his heart," she corrected him. "Sitting down to dinner won't hurt him in the least. He said he was sorry we weren't able to get away, after all, and he wants to spend time with us." She used her fingers to smooth a lock of hair away from his face. "I'm sure he can give your sister some very helpful ideas on starting a practice around here." Her fingers lingered against his cheek.

Jack couldn't evade the scent of her perfume curling around his face. He had once thought about telling her he honestly hated it. He found it too sickly sweet for his taste. He thought of the scent Casey wore. It didn't intrude, but beckoned.

It didn't take him more than two seconds to realize thinking about Casey wasn't a good idea right now.

Dammit, this was getting even more complicated. The new outrageous Casey was a strain enough on his nerves. What would she be like around Norton?

"I warned Casey that Daddy prefers a semiformal dinner," Nan chattered as she moved around the room, picking up a vase and setting it down an inch to the right. A lamp was likewise shifted. She picked up Jack's T-shirt strewn across the back of a chair and carefully folded it, then laid it back down. "He sounded so much more upbeat when I spoke with him. He said he felt as if the wedding gave him a new lease on life."

Jack offered her a comforting smile. He was well aware of Norton's physical condition, and the man would be lucky to live out the year.

"I just hope he hasn't gone to any trouble for this evening," he murmured. After all, Jack had enough trouble to go around.

"THERE'S MY CHILDREN!" Norton stepped out of the house with arms wide open to encompass both Nan and Jack. He favored his daughter with a kiss on the cheek and gave a pat on the back to Jack. He peered past them at the other two. "I can easily guess you're Jack's sister, Casey," he rumbled, reaching out to take her hand. "My dear, you are much too lovely for such a masculine name."

"But it's much easier to say than Cassandra," she said with a bright smile. "I'm very pleased to meet you, Mr. Xavier."

"Norton, please. We're all family here." He peered closely at Dan. "Who the hell are you?"

Dan's smile slipped a notch. He stuck out his hand. "It's good to see you again, Uncle Norton."

"You're not from my side of the family, are you?"

"Dan is Aunt Jessica's son, Daddy," Nan explained, clutching her father's arm. "Remember?"

His brow furrowed as he considered her explanation. "Jessica married that scientist, didn't she? The one who played with mice."

"He was in medical research," she corrected him.

Norton stared at Dan. "You don't look at all like your mother," he pronounced as if that was a plus. "Hope you're not anything like your father."

"I hate mice." Dan grinned. "Will that help?"

Norton shook his head. "A joker," he mumbled. "Let's all go inside." He walked in without bothering to see if they were following.

Jack deliberately took up the rear. Much as it pained him, he enjoyed watching Casey in another wonderfully revealing outfit. His revelry was interrupted when she looked over her shoulder and winked at him! He tripped on the last step and just barely saved himself from falling flat on his face.

"This is a special occasion that calls for only the

best,'' Norton announced, pouring champagne into crystal flutes and handing them out. He held up the last one. "To my darling daughter and her new husband. May they continue the Xavier dynasty." He smiled wryly. "Correction, Larson dynasty."

Casey's eyes met Jack's as she drank the bubbly liquid.

"I imagine your doctor wouldn't be happy with you toasting your daughter unless it was with sparkling water or cider," she said lightly. "I understand you haven't been well."

Norton chuckled. "My doctor learned a long time ago that I may listen to his suggestions, but that doesn't mean I always take them." He refilled his glass.

Casey walked over and plucked it out of his hand and set it to one side. "I'm sure he'd say that one glass would be acceptable, but more than one would be pushing it."

She could sense the tension coming from Nan and knew it could only mean one thing; no one ever told Norton Xavier what to do. Norton was the one to break the tension as his laughter echoed in the room.

"You are very definitely a doctor." He smiled at her. "Let me assure you I know my body better than any doctor."

Casey narrowed her eyes as she studied him. "You probably prefer golf to tennis and scotch on the rocks after a grueling game. Your blood pressure is high, not just because of your workload, but because you refuse to give up salt and fatty foods, and I just bet you couldn't properly end the day without your bed-time brandy.''

"Actually, I prefer cognac.'' Norton's gaze was shrewd as he viewed her. "You don't believe in pull-ing any punches, do you.''

"I have this idiosyncrasy,'' she said softly. "I like my patients to live.''

"I would think everyone would have that desire,'' Norton argued.

"Having the desire to live and having the guts to do whatever is necessary are two different things. I've learned that many people feel they don't need to fol-low rules to survive.'' Her gaze was steady as she locked eyes with him.

Norton's smile faltered. He turned to Jack. "Has she always been like this?'' he demanded.

Jack looked as if he was fighting back a grin. "She was much worse when she was younger,'' he replied. "Rumor had it when she was a resident she was well-known to lecture her patients that if they wanted to die to just ignore her, but if they wanted to live they had to listen to everything she said.''

"They didn't like my attitude,'' she admitted with a slight shrug. "But the majority of my patients fol-lowed my advice.''

Norton looked past Casey toward Dan, who lounged in a chair that had graced a French castle a couple of hundred years ago.

"If you don't want to turn out like your father,

you'll keep an eye on this woman," he boomed. "She's got guts." He turned back to Casey. "What's your handicap?"

She smiled. "I don't play golf."

"What? I'd think the damn AMA would drum anyone out of their organization if they didn't play golf."

"Honestly, Daddy, you're going to embarrass her," Nan scolded, jumping in before Casey could reply. "Casey hasn't been around us long enough to know what a tease you are. Not to mention a big softy."

"Soft like tempered steel," Casey said softly, moving away from Norton and over to a love seat. She sat down, crossing one leg over the other, causing her skirt to hike up another few inches.

"Daddy's looking better than he has in months," Nan said.

"I have to agree with that," Jack said, walking over to stand beside the chair Nan had seated herself in. She smiled and patted the chair arm with the silent suggestion he perch there. When he did just that, she grasped his hand and laced her fingers through his.

Casey was grateful her medical training had taught her to hide her emotions. Seeing her husband holding hands with another woman made her feel sick to her stomach. She couldn't believe she'd agreed to this farce. Heck, she'd actually initiated it by telling Nan she was Jack's sister.

Still, she had been gone three years. Jack had been told she was dead. She couldn't fault what he had done, but deep inside her she wished he had greeted her with open arms. Although, why she would have expected an effusive welcome was beyond her. Before she left, their marriage was lukewarm at best. If she had been asked to describe her marriage, she would have probably used the word *pleasant.*

But something had happened to her during the last three years. She'd seen marriages that were obviously based on passion by people who believed passion was necessary for the soul. She saw a love she couldn't even imagine experiencing. It left her yearning for that same kind of passion. While she had never felt it with Jonathon, she still never imagined finding it with another man.

Greg had tried to persuade her that they should consider themselves Adam and Eve and begin a new dynasty down there in the jungle. She hadn't wasted any time in setting him straight—while she greatly admired his mind, she had no desire for his body. Greg pouted for a time, but several nubile women in the village soon caught his attention. That hadn't stopped him from inferring he and Casey were much more than colleagues during those years with the villagers. She had sworn if she ever saw him again and if he said one word, she would make sure he remembered the black eye she'd given him. After that, he'd probably not bring up the subject again. She deliberately kept a pleasant smile pasted on her lips as she surveyed the group.

Norton sat in a high-backed chair that resembled a

throne. No wonder, since he seemed to enjoy acting like the ruler proudly overseeing his domain. For a man who had been rumored to be at death's door, he was looking remarkably spry this evening. Her gaze flickered over Jack, lingered, then moved on.

How did she even think she could treat him like a sibling? She knew that he couldn't start the day without brushing his teeth, even before having his shower and morning coffee. He drank hot tea when he had a cold, and he preferred boxer shorts to briefs. She knew the rough texture of his skin under her fingertips…the dark taste of his mouth when he kissed her…the feel of his hands on her bare skin….

She sat there, sensing the heat in her cheeks. She sipped her champagne in hopes the chilled liquid would equally cool her thoughts.

It didn't.

JACK HAD THE FEELING something was very wrong.

Sitting on his throne, Norton Xavier looked too chipper for a man who had been diagnosed terminally ill.

"So when will I see my first grandchild?" Norton asked.

Nan, who had been sipping her champagne, choked, and Jack could only sit there, stunned by the question.

"Daddy, give us some time," she murmured.

"I don't have any time," her father said bluntly.

"I'd like to know there will be a child to keep the business going."

"I thought you retired so you wouldn't have to worry about the business," Jack said lightly.

"I retired so my successor would have the time to get to know the business before I was gone," he told him. "But that didn't mean I'd stop thinking about it. Xavier Electronics has been going strong for two generations, and I don't intend to see it fail now."

"Considering Nan's ideas for further expansion, I don't think you'll have any worries," Jack assured him. "I've seen her proposals."

"You'll do fine, my boy," Norton exclaimed, ignoring Jack's words. "I know you will."

Jack smothered a curse. How long was it going to take for Norton to realize Nan had more than enough smarts to run the company? When Jack had agreed to take over the company, he thought Norton hadn't long to live and he planned to make sure everyone knew the true power was Nan. Obviously, the old man was going to make that difficult. Jack looked at Nan and couldn't miss the hurt shadowing her eyes.

"I plan to rely on Nan a lot to make the transition easier," Jack explained. "We'll make the perfect team, Norton. You'll see. As for now..." He held up his glass. "We came here for dinner and not to discuss business."

Norton threw back his head and laughed. "Jack, you're going to have to learn that there is never a wrong time to discuss business. I've always found it best when I get my victims sitting down and relaxed before I cut them off at the knees.''

"The hard line all the way," Casey murmured.

"That's right," he said forcefully. "If you want to be top dog, you've got to fight your way up there and do whatever is necessary to stay there." He nailed Dan with a steely gaze. "It sounds as if you need to learn that, boy."

Nan looked uncomfortable during her father's speech. She shifted her body in the chair, then stood up.

"I'm sure dinner is ready," she said in her musical hostess's voice. "Why don't we go into the dining room." She grasped Jack's hand and led the small parade out of the room.

Norton pushed himself out of his chair and approached Casey before Dan could realize what was going on.

"May I escort you in to dinner?" he asked with a courtly bow.

"Why, thank you, sir." She smiled as she accepted his arm.

"After dinner, I'll give you a list of people to see if you're opening your own practice here," he told her as they walked down the spacious hallway. "Or if you'd prefer to work in a well-established practice, I can guide you to the right contacts."

"Yes, I'm sure you can," Casey murmured.

She was right about dinner. Veal in a rich cream sauce, vegetables with cheese sauce. After eating an almost exclusively vegetarian diet for so long, she was finding it difficult to eat meat. She laughed to herself at the irony. It wasn't so long ago when she was back in the jungle craving a juicy cheeseburger with everything on it.

"You don't eat much, do you?" Norton said, gesturing with his fork.

"During my travels, meals weren't that important to my existence," she replied. "I also discovered I'm more alert if I don't overdo it with the evening meal."

Norton peered at her. She guessed he was also growing more farsighted and refused to admit it.

"You were the rebel in the family, weren't you."

She shook her head. "Actually, I was the model child," Casey said softly. "Tutors kept me occupied during the day, homework kept me out of mischief at night, and my weekends were spent with special projects."

She didn't appear uneasy that all eyes were on her.

"Actually, I was relieved when she had tutors," Jack said to break the charged silence. "Before that, she played hell with the grading curve in school. No one had a chance." He picked up his wineglass and toasted her. "But thanks to sis here, I passed calculus with flying colors."

Casey was grateful for Jack's intervention. She had no idea why she had blurted out what had always been private thoughts. She put it down to the champagne and vowed to never drink it again.

"So, Daniel," Norton boomed, "tell me what you've been up to since I saw you last."

"Daddy, Dan was seven years old then," Nan murmured.

"Fine, then just tell me what you've been doing for the past six months."

CASEY WAS NEVER SO relieved to see an evening end. True to his word, Norton Xavier took her aside after dinner and prepared a list of doctors and hospital administrators to visit. When she murmured something about a general practice, he immediately booed her words and talked to her about specialization. She could only think that for an electronics czar, he was well-informed about the medical community.

By the time she was settled in the back seat of Nan's Mercedes sedan, she felt a raging headache coming on. It didn't help that Dan was sitting much too close to her and his cologne was tickling her nose.

"Why don't we let the newlyweds have some time alone and go out to dinner tomorrow night," he suggested under his breath.

"I think I'll just spend a quiet evening catching up on things," she replied, tempted to plant her elbow in his midsection. For someone who was always so calm, she found herself thinking up fascinating methods of torture lately.

It was just a question whether she'd begin with Jack or Dan.

Judging from the gleam in Nan's eye as she looked at Jack, Casey decided her husband would benefit from her idea of torture first.

Chapter Five

Casey wanted nothing more than to sleep. Sleep was good for a headache. Sleep was good when it was after midnight.

But how could she sleep when there was tapping at the bedroom window?

She rolled over, muttered a few curses and wearily opened her eyes.

"Go 'way."

"We need to talk, Casey."

She opened her eyes again. "What is this, Jack? You've spent time with wife number two, so now you're here to give attention to wife number one. How democratic you are, dear." Her widemouthed yawn took out most of the sting in her sarcasm.

She could hear the sound of the screen slipping out of the window frame. She sat up in bed and rubbed her face with her fingertips. She watched Jack climb into the room and settle on the foot of the bed.

"Is there a reason why this couldn't wait until tomorrow?"

"It's not too easy to be alone with you with good old Cousin Dan hanging around," he grumbled, pulling up his legs and sitting cross-legged. "Don't turn on a light. Dan might see it as a signal from you."

Casey grimaced at the mention of the other houseguest. Dan had made his interest in her known almost right off the bat. She had done everything possible to indicate to him that interest wasn't returned, but he appeared to be blind when he wished.

"How long do you expect this to go on, Jack? Mr. Xavier doesn't seem as ill as he told you and Nan," she stated. "I don't like this at all."

"Think how I feel," he argued. "I don't know whether I'm coming or going. And treating you like a sister isn't all that easy, either."

"Really? Before I left for the jungle, there were plenty of times you treated me more like a sibling than a spouse," she said quietly.

Jack winced at the truth in her words. "If I did, it was because I felt you were treating me that way," he countered. "By the time you left on that trip, I felt as if we were more roommates than husband and wife."

Casey read the pain in his voice, which she knew was written on her face. "How sad we don't have a chance now to unravel the mess we made."

"True."

She lifted her head, her eyes glittering in the darkness.

"But then, we weren't given that chance, were

we?'' she said coldly. "You, obviously, had made other plans that didn't include me." She sat up, uncaring that the sheet fell to her waist. After all, it wasn't anything he hadn't seen before. Filling out the lacy front of her nightgown, her breasts rose and fell with each deep breath she took.

"I told you. Norton was dying and wanted to see Nan settled," he said around a clenched jaw. "He's one of the last chauvinists, and he insisted she marry a man who could run the company after his death. The thing is, Nan is the most qualified person to take over. And I intend to let her do just that."

"How kind of you," she drawled, her voice slicing him to ribbons. "I had no idea you had such a generous soul, Jonathon."

He bristled under her condescending tone. Generous, indeed. If only Jack could tell her how he practically owed his life to Norton Xavier. How he'd given Jack a reason to live when he believed Cassandra to be dead. But somehow Jack couldn't reveal the depth of his despair to Casey. She'd already told him it was no excuse. Instead, he simply said, "That's not fair."

"Whoever said life was fair?" Casey lifted her chin defiantly. "For the past three years I have lived without plumbing of any kind, using soap made from plant roots, eaten bugs and ended up with some pretty nasty parasites in my intestines off and on." She ignored his wince and continued, "I'd forgotten what it felt like to have a hot shower or a mattress under me. I came back here wondering how bad the culture shock was going to be. But I didn't worry because I knew you'd be there to help me through it." Her voice started to shake slightly, but she visibly shored herself up and went on. "I couldn't sleep my first night back because of all the sounds I hadn't heard in so long. The air smelled and tasted foul to me. The food was strange. I discovered so many things had changed while I was gone that I felt as if I'd landed on another planet." Her gaze bored into his with the intensity of a white-hot flame. "And the ones who helped me find my way back into this world were military psychologists and various scientists from the institute. Men and women who were more interested in what was going on in my mind than what was going on in my soul. I was suddenly afraid of fast cars, of people moving here and there, and of so much going on around me that had nothing to do with me. I was afraid it would all smother me. I—" Her voice started wavering again, and this time, she couldn't shore herself back up. She drew a deep breath and remained still as a statue. "I—"

Jack's breath caught in his throat. While he had been living the good life, she had been living under the most primitive conditions. And when she'd finally returned, she did so to a life that wasn't there for her. And a man who wasn't there for her.

He didn't stop to think. He uncoiled his legs and reached for her, taking her against his chest and settling her in his lap.

"Oh, Casey." Her name was a sigh on his lips. "I wish I had known earlier." He rested his chin against the side of her head.

"Why? You were busy changing your name, the entire way you look, living the fast life and getting engaged to a woman who's worth millions."

"Billions, actually, but that never had anything to do with it."

"If she wasn't so nice, I'd hate her." Casey pulled Jack's shirt out of his pants and wiped her eyes with the shirttail, then blew her nose. "*Bigamy* isn't a word in my vocabulary, not to mention it's not legal."

"All that matters is that Norton thinks we're married," he explained.

"Except Nan wants a real marriage." She wiped her eyes again.

"She only wants the appearance of one."

"Believe me, she wants *you*," Casey murmured, jabbing his chest with her forefinger. "Tonight she was looking at you as if you were a hot-fudge sundae and she had just come off a long diet."

Jack could hardly listen to her warning. His attention was more on the delicate line of her shoulders as her nightgown strap dropped down her arm. No tan line. Did this mean she was tanned all over? He had the right to ask the question, didn't he? Three years in the jungle. Thoughts of all the Tarzan movies he'd seen as a boy raced through his head. Jane seemed to wear less and less with each film....

He had no idea he was staring at her so intently until he noticed she was staring back at him similarly.

"You better go," she said in a rush.

He didn't move a muscle. "We have a lot to talk about."

"Yes, we do, but not here and not now."

Jack sat there, quiet and unmoving, his gaze locked with hers. The tension thickened between them until it seemed to surround them like a fog.

Finally Casey broke the silence. "Go back to your wife, Jack."

"You're my wife."

Her face could have been carved from marble. "Not tonight."

Muttering a curse, he slid off the bed and headed for the open doorway.

"Back the way you came in, Jack," she said quietly, her words arresting his escape.

Muttering yet another curse, he spun on his heel and climbed back out the window.

"Unpleasant dreams," he growled as he replaced the screen.

Casey lay back down in her bed. And twenty minutes later she was still punching her pillow as if she was actually punching Jack. With each shot, she muttered in a dark voice, "Damn you, Jack Larson."

CASEY'S SLEEP WASN'T restful nor were her dreams unpleasant. If anything, they were much too pleasant! She couldn't remember ever having the kind of

X-rated dreams she had last night. She mumbled curses against Jack as she made coffee as strong as possible. She wrinkled her nose at the bitter taste but gamely swallowed the dark brew.

She sat at the table with her coffee and a pad of paper so she could work on her résumé. When she finished, she studied her results.

"What a boring life I've led," she declared to herself, tapping her pen against the tabletop. "School and work. And now I'm considering going back to work."

"Then how about some playtime?" A male voice intruded on her self-evaluation.

Casey looked up to find Dan standing in the kitchen doorway. "Did you ever think about knocking?"

"Yes, thank you, I'd love some coffee." He swept a mug out of the cabinet and poured himself some. "Ugh!" He made a face. "Were you planning on floating any battleships in this?" He opened another cabinet door and rummaged around until he found a jar of nondairy creamer.

"There are times when that's all that will keep you awake when you're working a thirty-six-hour shift," Casey told him, holding up her cup.

Dan took the less-than-subtle hint and refilled her cup. "What are you doing?" He craned his head to look at the pad of paper.

"Working up a résumé," she replied. "I thought I'd see what the opportunities are around here."

"Norton—I mean Uncle Norton said he'd help you." Dan sat down across from her.

"I prefer looking on my own," she explained.

"The old man won't like you refusing his help," he warned.

"Just because everyone else gives in to him doesn't mean I have to." Casey heaved a deep sigh. "Is there a reason why you're here?"

Dan shrugged. "I thought you might like to go out for lunch and perhaps do some sight-seeing. I'm also very good at carrying packages if you want to do some shopping." He flashed his patented smile. "Maybe we could even take a drive down the coast," he murmured, his raised eyebrows indicating he wouldn't be adverse to anything she might have in mind.

Casey pulled several sheets of paper off the pad and handed them to him. "I have a better idea. Since you're talking about finding a job around here, why don't you work on your résumé?"

Dan didn't touch the paper. "Only if you promise to go swimming with me this afternoon."

"I don't make deals," she said loftily.

"Best way to get rid of me. I promise." He held two fingers up in a Boy Scout pledge.

Casey chuckled and shook her head. "Something tells me you weren't a Boy Scout."

"No, but I did know a lot of Girl Scouts."

CASEY MADE USE of Nan's home office computer to type up and print out her credentials. As promised, she examined Dan's résumé, made a couple of suggestions and relaxed by the pool blithely ignoring his blatant overtures.

"Why don't we find a private beach somewhere?" He sat on the end of her chaise longue.

She pushed at him with her foot until he almost fell off the chaise. "I like it here. Move. You're blocking my sun."

"You know, if you work on your new sister-in-law, who just happens to be extremely wealthy in her own right, you wouldn't have to worry about finances," Dan told her, folding his towel into a neat square and sitting down on it. "She's very generous."

Casey kept her eyes closed. She knew if she looked at Dan she'd be tempted to hit him and ruin his obviously expensive orthodontic work.

"I prefer earning my own keep," she said in an even voice.

He trailed his fingers across her thigh, glistening with suntan oil.

She lifted her sunglasses a scant inch to glare at him. "Dan, I said I'd come out here and keep you company, not let you play Braille on my thigh. Go for a swim and cool off."

"Come with me."

"I'm busy."

Dan got to his feet and looked down at her. "Then, I guess there's only one thing I can do." He swooped down and picked her up in his arms. "And that's take you with me!" he shouted, running for the pool.

"Game playing?" A cool male voice intruded just as Dan was preparing to drop her into the water.

Casey swiveled her head to see Jack standing on the edge of the patio with Nan beside him. Both didn't look happy about what they saw.

"Put me down," Casey ordered under her breath.

"Okay." Dan grinned. He opened his arms but Casey held on tightly and pulled Dan into the cool water with her.

Casey instantly regretted having an open mouth as chlorine-tainted water filled her mouth. She bobbed to the surface choking and gagging.

"You idiot!" she gasped, paddling her way to the side. She held on to the coping and shook her head to get her hair out of her face.

"What kind of moronic trick was that?" Jack demanded of Dan as he walked over to the side of the pool. He squatted down and offered his hand to Casey. She grasped his wrist with a tight grip as he hauled her out of the pool.

"Darling, aren't you going a little overboard about them playing in the pool?" Nan asked with a tight smile curving her lips.

"Not when he's doing something dangerous to my sister," he growled, clapping Casey on the back.

"I'm not choking!" she insisted in between coughs. "But I will be if you keep it up." She shrugged off his hand.

"Where the hell is the rest of your suit?"

Casey's head whipped back and forth as she tried to conquer the ringing in her ears from Jack's shout.

"If you're trying to deafen me, you're doing an admirable job," she said crossly. "What is your problem now?" She jumped when Jack pulled her towel off the chaise and draped it around her waist to hide the scraps of hot pink silk that just barely kept her from being arrested for indecent exposure.

"Your entire butt is showing," he growled, glowering at Dan, whose grin slipped.

"It's a thong bikini, Jack. It's supposed to show," she said in slow, measured tones, whipping the towel off. Within seconds, he had snatched it out of her hand and tried to put it around her waist again, but had no luck as she moved away from him.

"Heavens, Jack, Casey's no longer a child her big brother can boss around," Nan said, walking up to them. She looped her arm through his. Her smile wasn't as bright when she faced Dan. "Have you spent the afternoon swimming?"

"I tried to work on my tan until your cousin decided to get funny," Casey grumbled. She glared at Dan. "Let me get something straight. I hate people throwing me into a pool, and I don't like people dropping me into a pool, either. If you do it again, I promise you will feel pain in parts of your body you didn't even know you had."

"I was just having some fun," he argued.

"That kind of fun I don't like." She ran her fingers

through her hair, slicking it back from her face. "I
told you I only wanted to work on my tan. If I wanted
to swim, I would have gone in the pool by myself."
Swinging her towel by her side, she walked away.

Jack didn't want to look at the appealing sight of
Casey's almost bare body. Her rear cheeks were the
same uniform bronze as the rest of her. *Didn't they
wear any clothing at all in the Amazon?* Is that what
Greg had seen?

"Jack, what's wrong?"

It wasn't until Nan's question interrupted him that
he realized the whimper he'd heard was his own.

"I APOLOGIZE FOR JACK'S behavior." Nan handed
Casey a glass of flavored sparkling water. They sat
on the patio while the men were watching over the
food on the barbecue. "I have no idea what got into
him."

Casey had an idea what, but she wasn't about to
divulge that thought to the other woman. *Other
woman.* Wryly, she wondered who truly was the other
woman in this comedy of errors. She finally decided
it was best if they shared the role. No reason why she
should be the only one to suffer. The only problem
was Nan didn't have her first husband lurking around.

"I guess he prefers to forget that his little sister is
all grown up," she drawled, resting the chilled glass
against her cheek. She hadn't missed the hot look in
Jack's eyes when he saw the brevity of her bathing

suit. That was why she took her time choosing something "appropriate" for dinner that evening after Nan had asked her to join them. She lifted her face, enjoying the cool ocean breeze. The sound of the ocean on one side warred with the music coming out of discreetly placed speakers in the patio area.

"I did something useful today by listing my credentials and making a few calls to see if there were any openings," she said. "I even helped Dan write his résumé. All I can say is the man can't spell to save his life."

"Daddy said he would put you in touch with people," Nan reminded her.

"Let me make this clear, Nan. I don't want anyone to say I'm using you," she said bluntly. "I've always been able to do very well on my own."

"Believe me, no one can use Daddy. He offered because he likes you and wants to see you in the best position possible." She smiled. "I think he likes you because you stand up to him. Very few people do that."

"I've always been known for speaking my mind," Casey admitted. "But it's only been the past few years that I've decided life is short and I may as well say what I mean. I don't try to be hurtful, but I won't lie, either."

"Like Jack," Nan said softly, watching her groom with a wistful expression in her eyes. "He told me he'd never lie to me and he never has."

Casey wasn't sure where this conversation was

heading, but she did know one thing. She didn't want to hear Nan's private feelings or any confessions she might be compelled to make.

"So you're saying I'm actually doing Norton a favor in allowing him me to help me out," Casey said, in hopes of steering clear of any private confidences.

"Of course. He loves to help his family."

"Just as long as he realizes that doesn't mean he'll have free medical care," she quipped.

Nan laughed. "That is something you'll definitely have to tell Daddy." She leaned forward and touched Casey's arm. "He and Jack are a lot alike. They both enjoy helping people. If it wasn't for Jack, I wouldn't have this chance to show the board of directors what I can do. He's a lifesaver."

Casey's smile was strained, at best. "Yes, Jack is just a Boy Scout all grown up."

"THEY SURE GET ALONG good, don't they?" Dan commented, using his beer can to gesture toward Casey and Nan.

"Yes, they do," Jack replied, uncomfortable with the idea of what they might be talking about.

The day hadn't been one of the best. Sleep had been spotty, at best. How was he expected to sleep with the memory of Casey in a nightgown that showed more than it covered up? How could he sleep when all he thought about was what she looked like and smelled like. He was only thankful that Nan had continued to occupy the other room. She had smiled and told him she realized he would need a few nights to recuperate from his illness. He had lain in his bed, staring at the ceiling and wishing he was back in the guest house. He silently berated himself for not following through and kissing Casey, but he also had the feeling if he had done that she wouldn't have thought twice about hitting him.

Feeling groggy from his restless sleep, he had driven in to work with Nan with the intention of making sure those in the know understood she was the one in charge, not him. There had been a round of meetings, sly questions as to why the newlyweds hadn't gone away for a honeymoon, and as if that wasn't enough, they'd come home early to find Casey and Dan playing in the swimming pool like a couple of teenagers with overloaded hormones! Then he saw the scant excuse for a bathing suit Casey wore and he thought he would explode in millions of tiny pieces.

He didn't remember her body being that curvy three years ago! Nor did he remember her ever wearing anything that seductive. Not even to bed. But then the Casey he was seeing now wasn't the Cassandra of three years ago. The woman he married made his heart speed up when he would see her, but now his heart raced into overdrive. And it had nothing to do with the slipdress she was now wearing, either.

"You know, you didn't have to pull the protective brother routine today," Dan murmured as he sipped his beer. "Casey is safe with me."

Jack speared him with his gaze. "She's going through a rough time right now. The last thing she needs is some guy on the make running after her."

Dan's brows rose with surprise. "You're making me sound as if I have no scruples."

"If the shoe fits," Jack murmured, flipping the chicken breasts over.

Dan's features tightened with a swift burst of anger. He stared down at the beer can he'd almost crushed in his hand. "Nan could have had her choice of any man in this state," he said in a low voice. He lifted his head. "But then she had to limit that choice to someone dear old Dad would approve of. And for the life of me, I can't figure out why he approves of you."

"Maybe it's because I have scruples."

There was no telling how long their staring contest would have gone on if Nan hadn't walked over to ask them how long before the chicken was ready.

"You have two hungry women over there," she teased.

Dan's expression turned playful as he faced her. "Don't you worry, ma'am," he drawled. "We captured some mighty fine vittles for you ladies."

Nan laughed at his foolishness but Jack merely rolled his eyes.

"Then, Tex, why don't you mosey on into the house and get a platter for the chicken," he suggested with a decided bite in his voice.

Dan sketched a mocking salute and sauntered into the house.

"Jack, are you and Dan having problems?" Nan asked, watching his retreating figure.

"Let's just say I don't like his happy-go-lucky attitude," he muttered.

"Nor that he's interested in your sister."

Jack could almost detect an odd note in her voice.

"Perhaps it would have been better if I hadn't asked him to stay," she said with faint apology in her voice.

He shook his head. "Don't worry about it." His mouth twisted in a smile. "We don't have an orthodox marriage, so why shouldn't our relatives descend on us right away? Are there any more cousins due to show up?" he asked, hoping to lighten the mood.

Nan chuckled. "I promise no more cousins if you promise no more sisters."

"I can safely promise that."

She shook her head. "I swear, Jack, you act as if she's your wife more than your sister." She patted his arm before walking to the house. "I think I'll see why Dan is taking so long with the platter."

Jack heaved a deep sigh as he moved the chicken around on the grill so it wouldn't burn.

"Having one wife too many is sheer hell."

Chapter Six

Jack couldn't sleep. In the end, he grabbed a bottle of water out of the minifridge in his room and walked out onto the small balcony. His view of the ocean was tempting, but the view of the guest house far to the left was even more tempting. There, he could see a small light in the back that he knew came from the bedroom. Casey's bedroom. It seemed she couldn't sleep, either.

If he'd been a man, he would have told Nan the truth tonight. He would have told her that their marriage wasn't valid because Casey was still his wife. He would have told her he wanted to go off somewhere where he and Casey could rediscover each other. And he would have, too, if Nan hadn't said those fateful words before they retired to their respective bedrooms.

"Thank you for giving me this chance, Jack," she had murmured, pressing a kiss on his cheek. "Thank you for letting me show Daddy I can handle it."

That took the wind right out of his confession. Instead, he went to bed hating himself for keeping silent.

So now he stood on the balcony, drinking the chilled water and thinking of his wife sleeping alone.

Jack felt his lower body stirring at the thought of Casey in bed. Was she wearing that nightgown that covered so little? Or did she own more scraps of silk and lace fashioned like that one? He drank more water in hopes it would cool off his libido, but it didn't seem to be doing any good. He had the idea he would be better off drowning in the damn stuff.

Jack cursed softly and dropped the water bottle when the soft ring of his bedside phone interrupted his thoughts. At first, he was tempted to ignore it. By the fourth ring, he decided to answer it before Nan knocked on his door and asked what was wrong.

He snatched up the receiver. "Yes?"

"Did I wake you?"

He dropped onto the side of the bed. Maybe dreams can come true, after all.

"Considering how long you let it ring, I'd say you were hoping to wake me up," he said. "Sorry, Casey, I was still awake."

Her soft chuckle warmed his ear. "I thought so. You never enjoyed being awakened and tended to snarl when the phone rang in the middle of the night. I didn't disturb Nan, did I?"

"If it will make you feel better, I'll snarl like a tiger," he offered, punching up his pillows behind his back. "And as for your comment about Nan, she's in the next room and probably sleeping like a baby."

"Mmm, go for it. Just don't wake up the baby."

Jack immediately focused on something else he'd like to go for. Something that would give him a great reason to snarl. Such as the woman wearing silk and lace.

"How did you know my extension?" he asked instead.

"There's a nice little phone directory down here with extension numbers for the house. My, my, it's like calling the White House without having to go through a main switchboard," she told him. "I wanted to give you a chance to apologize for your beastly behavior this afternoon."

"Beastly behavior? The man had you in his arms ready to throw you in the pool. I see it more as defending your virtue," he argued, still seeing that picture in his mind.

"That would have been difficult to do since you already took that years ago."

Jack felt his midsection tighten until he felt as if steel encased him. What kind of spell was she weaving around him?

"Jack, are you still there?" Her soft voice traveled over him like millions of tiny fingers.

"Yeah," he croaked. "Fine, you want an apology. You apologize for going outside in that sorry excuse for a bathing suit and showing everything off to

Reynolds and I'll apologize for trying to protect you."

"I've had better apologies, but I'll settle for that," Casey murmured. "Actually, I thought you'd like my suit. I have learned that wearing little clothing freed the spirit."

"Well, your spirit was freed, all right." He fumbled for the nightstand drawer. He'd given up smoking a year ago, but now was the perfect time to begin again.

"I made some calls today about finding a position in the area. Is that going to bother you? My working around here?"

Everything about you bothers me.

"No, it wouldn't bother me," he lied. "I know how important your work is to you. I've heard the university has an excellent medical school and a highly-thought-of medical research department."

He could hear the soft rustle of her body moving under the sheets. He wished he was lying beside her.

"I don't intend to go back to teaching or research, Jack. I'm going back to active practice. The past three years has taught me that working directly with the patients is what I need to do." She spoke in a low voice that was sending all sorts of ideas to his brain, along with the southern regions of his body.

"So everything you said to Norton about general practice was legitimate."

"Every word," she replied. "I used to think I couldn't interact with patients. That's why I resorted to teaching, but when push came to shove, I learned that I could do it. And I enjoyed it.''

''Norton's right. General practice won't pay the way specialization would.''

''I'd have to go back and take additional training after I decided what specialty I'd want,'' she protested. ''With general practice I'd have variety. If anything, my second choice would be emergency medicine, but I know I'd need a great deal of additional training for that.''

Jack smiled. He wanted to tell her he always knew she had that ability. He was just glad she'd finally discovered it. ''Then I say, go for it.''

''I'm also going to be looking for a place of my own.'' She paused, letting her words sink in. ''It's not a good idea for me to stay here very long.''

He was stunned. He wanted to tell her he'd just found her again and she was already leaving him. But then, he'd given away that right.

''Nan will try to talk you out of it.''

''I'll tell her I need privacy. She'll understand.'' Her sheets rustled again, and he was positive he could smell her perfume. ''I should let you sleep.''

He settled back against his pillows. ''If you're seeing people tomorrow, you're the one who will need her beauty sleep.''

''I did learn one thing, Jack,'' Casey murmured. ''I don't sleep as well when I'm alone. Good night.'' A soft click indicated she'd hung up.

Jack's hand was shaking when he tried to replace

the receiver, but it took more than one try. He grabbed one of his pillows and jammed it over his face. His groan was a combination of pain and frustration.

"If I had a pair of ruby slippers, I would tap my heels three times, and my world would return to the way it should be."

CASEY HAD GONE TO SLEEP hoping she had left Jack unsettled. She knew she had been. For a woman who always considered her sex drive minimum at best, she seemed to be constantly thinking about sex every time she saw Jack or thought about him.

With the intention of setting up appointments, she dressed conservatively.

She was walking out of the guest house wearing a trim copper linen suit when a black limousine rolled up in front of her.

Casey stopped, curious to see who the visitor was, when the passenger window rolled downward and Norton's face appeared.

"Good girl," he said with an approving wave of his cigar. "Get in."

"Did we have an appointment?" she asked sweetly.

He frowned. "Nan said you were going out today to make some contacts. We're having lunch with the chief of surgery with Oceanview Medical Center. So get in." He pushed the door open.

Casey's brows rose. She had already learned that

Oceanview was one of the top medical centers around. She didn't move to get in.

"How kind of you to ask me if I'd be interested." She stepped into the limo and settled back on cushions that felt soft as a cloud. "You really should think about taking some courses in self-confidence, Norton. You might discover that you can go out and face the world without fear." She stared at the cigar and raised an eyebrow.

He chuckled and promptly tamped it out. "My grandfather would say you have a lot of moxie."

She inclined her head in silent thanks. "It took me a while to discover that as long as I don't hurt anyone with my words, I may as well speak my mind. So tell me, why did you set up this lunch? What strings are you attaching?"

"None," he protested. "I thought I'd give you a chance to see the finest in the area. Gerald isn't a stupid man. He'll see you have just what he needs."

A chilling thought occurred to Casey. She hated to even voice it.

"Did you have me investigated?" she asked in a voice that boded ill for him if he gave the wrong answer.

"And have you use a rusty scalpel on me? I just asked someone in the medical field about a Dr. Larson and learned you were attending medical school when most girls were out losing their virginity," he said bluntly. "It seems you used to teach and do research, then you dropped out of sight after working with a scientific institute that set up medical centers in indigent Third World countries. What exactly did you do during that time?''

"I guess you could say I made a small part of the world a little nicer,'' she said evenly. "Doctors are needed all over the world, Norton. More in some areas than others. I decided it wouldn't hurt to do my part. Admittedly, I got more than I expected, but it was worth it.''

Norton eyed her the same way he had at his house. Again, Casey didn't look away.

"You and your brother aren't all that much alike.''

"Not where it counts.'' She continued smiling.

"What was his wife like?''

Casey's smile didn't slip, although she felt a hitch deep in her heart.

"She was an introvert who had trouble interacting with the outside world, and she was happier with the scientific world,'' she replied softly. "She wasn't an easy person to get to know, but I felt she was a good wife to Jack. They were a happy couple. Admittedly, I didn't see a lot of them, even though the three of us worked at the same university. We were all caught up in our own departments.''

"Jack said very little about her,'' he said. "His grief over her death was still very strong when he arrived out here. As a widower myself, I told him that only time would take care of his pain, but he had to go on. I admit I may have done more than my part in pushing Nan at him, but I had my reasons. She

needs someone steady like Jack. I knew if they spent
enough time together they'd discover just how com-
patible they are.'' He seemed to preen, as if waiting
for praise for his matchmaking.

Casey tipped her head to one side, studying him
not as a doctor might, but as a woman. ''Norton, you
are a very naughty boy. You like to make sure people
around you dance to your tune, don't you? No matter
that it might not be what they've planned for their
lives, as long as it's what you want. That's not a good
idea, because it could really backfire on you.''

''Not with Jack and Nan,'' he said with smug confidence. ''That boy needed a wife and a reason to get
on with his life. I gave him both.''

Casey turned away from him. She had a sneaking
hunch that his heart attack wasn't as serious as he'd
let on. And he'd used it to his advantage to rein Jack
in. She knew Jack had no idea what had been done,
but she did wonder what Nan knew about it. Casey
couldn't imagine the other woman would be a part of
such a plan, but she had to admit she didn't know her
very well. She made a mental note to change that.

''And now that you're out here, I plan to make sure
you find a good life for yourself,'' Norton continued.

''Norton, let me make things perfectly clear. I
promise not to embarrass you at lunch. And I promise
to listen with an open mind, but if I do take any position you led me into and I later discover there are
strings attached, I will get out that rusty scalpel of

mine and use it where it will hurt most," she promised with a soft coo in her voice.

Norton winced and laughed, as if she had told him a wonderful joke. But the look in his eye told her he knew she was speaking the truth.

CASEY HAD TO ADMIT lunch wasn't as bad as she feared it would be. Norton appeared to know exactly what he was doing. He introduced Casey to Dr. Gerald Montgomery, then sat back and let nature take its course as the conversation soon turned to medicine.

Casey liked the no-nonsense man, and she could see he was a doctor who cared about his patients. What a shame his patients were ones who paid extremely high fees for his caring nature. She accepted an invitation to view the medical center the following day and returned to the limo with Norton, who wore a grin the width of the Cheshire cat's.

"Don't send out the wedding invitations just yet," she warned him. "I only agreed to look over the medical center. Not move into the corner office and see patients that afternoon."

"Once you see the center and hear what they can offer you, you'll be ready to hire a decorator for your new office," he said confidently. He glanced out the smoked glass window. "How would you like to stop by the company? You can see what your brother does, although why they didn't take off for their honeymoon, I'll never know. Jack's going to be pretty busy once that new contract is finalized."

"A philosophy professor turned manufacturing magnate," she mused. "Somehow the two don't go together very well."

"They do if that professor is trained by one of the best."

Casey shook her head. "We really need to work on your confidence."

Norton laughed as he instructed the driver to take them by the company.

Casey wasn't sure what she was expecting, but a company that took up enough acres for a national park wasn't it. Buildings sprawled everywhere, surrounded by a high fence with several gates manned by armed guards, who checked everyone going in and out.

"You have to have good security when you've got defense contracts," Norton explained after the guard waved them through. "We set up state-of-the-art security measures to keep those contracts. We have a day-care center, a fully equipped infirmary and a helicopter for emergencies."

"All right, you're impressing me already," she admitted, "but I'd like to know where the hotel and casino are."

He shook his head at her glib remark. "Did you always have this mouth?"

"Only for the last few years, but I've liked it so much I decided to keep it." She smiled at the driver as he helped her out of the car.

Norton escorted her inside to the reception desk.

He reached over and plucked a badge from the desktop while Casey looked around curiously. Wine-colored couches and chairs for vendors and visitors. Coffee tables holding business periodicals and a scattering of telephones.

"She doesn't need to sign in," he told the receptionist.

"But, sir, it's one of your firmest rules," she protested, wide-eyed.

"And a good one," Casey agreed, picking up a pen and scrawling her name in the visitor log.

"Is it required for all you doctors to have such terrible handwriting?" Norton asked.

"Absolutely." She pinned the badge to her breast pocket and followed him down the hallway to a bank of elevators. Norton chose the farthest one, stepped inside and inserted a key before pressing the button for the executive floor. "Is this like a key to the executive washroom?" she asked.

He smiled and shook his head. "Let's just call it an express elevator," he explained.

When the doors slid silently open, Casey viewed plush amber carpeting and furniture that could only be genuine antiques. She sincerely doubted Norton would allow fakes into a company that was obviously his pride and joy.

"Marcia," he greeted the young woman seated behind an elegant writing table. The only modern concession was a discreet earphone with a wire attached to a telephone system fastened to the underside of the desk. "You're looking lovely today. By any chance, is my son-in-law and daughter available?"

"I'm sure they are, Mr. Xavier." She smiled brightly even as her fingers tapped in a series of numbers. She spoke softly into the attached mouthpiece and looked up. "Go on in, Mr. Xavier."

"Thank you, Marcia." He strode down a hallway.

Casey glanced at the artwork on the walls that suited the antique furniture. "Are all the offices decorated like this?"

He shook his head. "I like my people to feel individual. Up here they're given a budget to decorate their office any way they wish."

"Norton, my dear, you must be worth a lot of money," Casey purred impudently. "My, my, what a catch you are."

He chuckled as he opened the door at the end of the hallway and stepped inside without knocking. When it swung open, they found Jack and Nan seated in a corner of the large room, where a serving tray was set with a carafe and china cups.

"Daddy, what a surprise." Nan stood up and walked over to her father, pressing a kiss against his cheek.

"I thought I'd show Casey what her brother does all day," Norton announced as he nodded toward Jack. "We just had lunch with Gerald Montgomery."

Nan's eyes widened. "Casey, are you going to join the medical center staff? They only take the best there."

"I haven't decided yet," she admitted as she glanced at Jack, who had stood up when they entered. He looked dapper in a dark blue suit with a white-and-navy pin-striped shirt and blue tie. She decided he looked just as good dressed up as he did in casual clothing. To keep her mind off just how good he looked, she glanced around the office.

"Norton." Jack shook his hand. "Are you sure you're not just using Casey as an excuse so you can check up on us?" he joked.

"It's nice to see that big brother is busy working." Casey smiled sweetly. "Although, I thought sitting around and drinking coffee was only done in television commercials. So this is where you play the head man." She walked up to the bank of windows that made up one wall. "Quite a view," she said while looking out.

Casey could sense Jack's presence the moment he walked up to stand behind her. From the other side of the room, she could hear Norton asking Nan questions and her soft-voiced replies.

"So you decided to let Norton find a practice for you?" he murmured in a voice low enough so they wouldn't be overheard.

She didn't turn around. "Why not? I could learn to play golf, work three days a week and still make a lot of money catering to people who have more money than they know what to do with."

"And here you were talking about the joy you received in caring for natives whose idea of wealth must have been a two-room hut. You know, sometimes I wondered if you hadn't stayed in research and teaching because you didn't want to deal with real life. Now I realize it also gave you a lot of prestige, what with you being so young.''

"Beware of throwing stones, Jonathon." Her soft voice was coated with fine-tempered steel. "You're already living in a house built with lies. If you're not careful, it will all fall down around you."

"Damn you, Casey. Maybe it would have been better if you hadn't come back at all,'' he growled before striding away.

"Maybe it would have," she whispered to herself, looking out the window but not seeing a thing.

CASEY DIDN'T REMEMBER the tour of the compound. She assumed she made the right responses, since Norton didn't appear to notice a difference in her. She was never so glad as when she was deposited back at the house.

"You make sure to call Gerald first thing in the morning," Norton told her before he took his leave. "I'm glad to see Jack's side of the family has gumption. I sure never see it with Nan's mother's side." He kissed her on the cheek and climbed back in his limousine.

"Thank you for lunch!" she called after him. And breathed a deep sigh of relief when he was gone. She was also relieved to see Dan's Porsche was gone.

"Maybe he's looking for a job." She shook her head. "What was I thinking?"

Casey walked into the guest house with the intention of changing into her bathing suit and taking a swim to clear her head. She hoped it would work.

"JACK, ARE YOU EVEN listening to me?"

He winced at the impatience in Nan's voice. "Yes," he lied.

She stood in front of him with her hands braced on her hips and a frown marring her lovely features. "Then what did I say?" she demanded.

He winced again. "There's a problem with our supplier in Little Rock."

"Kansas City."

"That's right," he nodded. "A problem with our supplier in Kansas City."

She let loose with an exasperated sigh. "Jack, one of us will have to fly out there and get this matter settled."

"It should be you," he said. "You know more about what's going on out there than I do."

"Why don't we both go?" she suggested, perching a hip on the edge of the desk with her legs crossed. Her top leg swung gently against his knee as he sat to one side. "They're going to expect you to appear."

"Which is exactly why you should go," Jack insisted. "Let them find out right off the bat that they deal with you or they don't deal with us at all."

Nan's smile broadened. "You want me to be bad?" she asked with a purr in her voice.

Jack felt a tightening deep in his gut. He managed a smile when Nan's forefinger trailed across the top of his knee.

His wife was trying to seduce him right here in the office where anyone could just walk in!

He'd remembered once reading that danger put an edge to lovemaking, which made it more erotic and arousing. For him, it was just the opposite. Especially when the woman coming on to him wasn't his wife and the scent of his real wife's perfume still lingered in the room.

Nan obviously sensed his uneasy manner and drew back. She cocked an eyebrow as she gazed at him. "Honestly, Jack, we're married," she teased. "It's allowed."

"Not when someone could walk in," he muttered, pushing himself out of the chair.

Nan rose to her feet and walked around the desk. "I doubt anyone would walk in without announcing himself first." She started to pour herself a cup of coffee, then paused and turned around. "Jack, is everything all right?"

"Of course. Why?" He struggled not to let any panic into his voice.

"Because you haven't acted like yourself since the wedding. Are you regretting this?"

Jack stood up and walked over to her. He smiled and cupped her cheek with his palm. "Any man who would regret being with you should have a reality check." He kissed her lightly. "Now, if the boss doesn't mind, I'm heading for my office to pretend to do some work. As for anything else, we need to set an example for the staff. If we're caught chasing each other around the office, pretty soon they'll all think they can do it and then where would we be?"

"Happier?" she murmured as she watched him leave.

"I REALLY HATE TO LEAVE at this time. I'd hoped we could find the time to get to know each other better," Nan said, leading Casey into her dressing room that adjoined a walk-in closet the size of most bedrooms. Two open suitcases were laid out. "I hope you don't mind if we talk while I pack?"

"Not at all." Casey was enjoying herself poking through Nan's closet. Clothes were neatly arranged according to season, color and occasion. There were racks of shoes and drawers for lingerie and accessories. "Do you actually wear everything in here?" She pulled out a powder blue satin gown with a sequined bodice.

Nan grimaced. "Not really, but I never seem to have time to shop when I need something, so I use a personal shopper."

"No bored-socialite life for you," Casey commented, putting the gown back.

"Oh, I did live that life. I shopped and lunched and saw my hairdresser twice a week, facials twice a week, had my nails done and assisted on all the right charity events." Nan shook her head, still amazed at her former life-style. "I was soon so bored I thought I would scream. So I started talking to Daddy about his work. I'm sure he was patronizing me in the beginning, but he soon discovered that my business degree was more than a piece of paper. But while I knew what was necessary and proved I could do the work, it wasn't enough for him." She sat down on the bed, folding and refolding a nightgown. "I didn't have the Y chromosome."

"Your father is a true chauvinist," Casey agreed. "I think if he had his way, we'd all be in the kitchen barefoot and pregnant. So, with the way I cook, he'd either starve to death or die of food poisoning."

Nan giggled at her flip remark. "You can't cook?"

"I can toss a mean salad and heat up soup from a can," she freely admitted. "And in a pinch I can whip up pudding."

"Then, no one will say you lure men with your cooking," she chuckled.

Casey's smile froze on her lips. She hurriedly buried her face in a stack of sweaters, each lovingly folded with tissue paper between the folds.

"I guess I'm just not the type men like," she mumbled, fingering a cream-colored sweater.

"When I get back, I'm going to throw you into the social circle," Nan declared, standing up and laying the nightgown into the suitcase. "I know lots of men who would enjoy getting to know you better, and I intend to introduce you to all of them.''

"Introduce who?" Jack walked in.

Nan smiled and walked over to kiss him on the cheek. "I told Casey we need to introduce her to some of the eligible men we know. She needs to find someone who will appreciate her."

Jack looked over his shoulder at Casey, who flashed a bright smile at him. She was the picture of innocence.

"Casey isn't here to meet men," he blurted.

"Why not?" Casey said, keeping her tone matter-of-fact. "It's been a while and—"

"I don't want to hear it!" He held up his hand to stop her words. His dark gaze bored into her like a laser. "You said you're planning to return to work. I'd concentrate on that first."

Casey picked up a filmy teddy that was the color of candlelight and shook it out, idly putting it in front of her as she studied herself in the mirror.

"One thing that I've always prided myself on is my ability to concentrate on more than one thing and give both my full attention," she said brightly, turning around with the teddy still held in front of her. "Where did you get this, Nan? Do you know if they have it in other colors?"

"Why don't you take it?" Nan declared. "I can see that would look better on you than me."

"Oh, I couldn't," she cooed. "But I will. Jack, isn't it pretty?"

His face was a dark red, and he seemed to look everywhere but at her. "Great, just great."

"I'm certainly glad you have more enthusiasm for my lingerie, darling," Nan murmured with a secret smile.

Casey took one look at Jack. She was tempted to throw the teddy at him. She was tempted to cut his heart out. And she'd make sure he was wide-awake for the entire procedure. Of course, after she pulled out his heart with her bare hands, she'd work on a few other choice parts of his anatomy with the dullest and rustiest scalpel she could find.

"Jack," she said softly.

"What?" he asked warily.

"Eat dirt and die."

Chapter Seven

"Eat dirt and die?" Jack charged into the guest house. "Why the hell did you say something as ridiculous as that?"

Casey looked up from her book, which rested lightly on her abdomen. She was lying on the couch with bare legs crossed at the ankles and a glass of Diet Coke and bowl of cheese-flavored crackers within reach.

"Probably because I felt it would be something a baby sister would say to her autocratic older brother. It seemed to fit my image."

"Yeah, the image of a brat. *Hey!*" He ducked just in time when a book sailed past him. "What the hell was that for?" Jack stared at her as if he thought she'd lost her mind.

She sat up. "That was for the way you used to try to patronize me when we were first married."

"*What?*" He threw up his hands. "*I* patronized *you?* The woman who could stare down university heads without breaking a sweat. The woman who calmly informed one of the medical school's largest benefactors that the kind of medical attention he wanted wasn't what he needed. I couldn't patronize you if my life depended on it," he stated with quiet fury. "*You* were the one who made *me* feel as if I never got past the third grade."

"Oh, please!" Casey rolled her eyes. "You have more self-confidence than anyone I know. Well, perhaps not more than Norton," she quickly amended her statement. "But pretty close. Don't try to claim I could intimidate you." She flashed him the glare that had easily turned other men to cinders.

Jack sat down in the chair facing her. "Which is why you threw a book at me."

"No, I threw a book at you because I hated the way you treated me. The way you've treated me since I came here." She leaned forward, pounding her fist into her opposite hand to make her point. "It's insane here as it is. What you're doing is making it worse."

"Me?" he burst in. "I'm not the one who's walking around here swinging her hips and showing off her body."

Casey stared at him as if she couldn't believe what she was hearing. "Swinging her hips..." She couldn't hold it back any longer. She bent forward laughing so hard she had to wrap her arms around her stomach. "I'm not only accused of intimidation tactics but of acting like an overage Lolita." She gasped, still trying to catch her breath, but her laughter refused to stop. She looked up, took one look at the fierce expression on his face and immediately started howling again. "All right," she said, giggling, holding up her hand. "I'll calm down."

"I'm glad you think it's funny," he said stiffly, sitting there just as stiffly.

Casey erupted in another spate of giggles. Under Jack's deadly glare, she finally took several deep breaths until she could control her mirth.

"I bet you just wow them in the boardroom with those looks," she said. "Is that what you used on the unruly students in your classes?"

He refused to unbend. "Only when necessary. I can't believe you threw a book at me."

"I would have felt better about it if you hadn't ducked in time," she grumbled. She swung around and stretched out her legs, propping her feet on the coffee table. "Even if it would have hurt a perfectly good book."

Jack leaned over and picked up the book.

"Already boning up on surgical techniques?" He held it up.

"I thought I'd check out new ways to cut out someone's heart with little muss and fuss," she said pleasantly. "Of course, if you died during the procedure we'd have a little trouble with the funeral. Who do you think will be considered the official widow?"

He winced. "All right, this was the most ridiculous stunt I could have pulled. But dammit, I was told you were dead! I had thought of myself as a widower for almost three years!''

''A missing person cannot be declared legally dead until seven years has passed,'' she pointed out. ''I'm curious, Jack. What proof did they give you of my death, since they obviously didn't have a body to show you.'' She looked expectantly for his reply.

He shifted uneasily in his chair. ''They found what little had been left of your camp.''

She nodded. ''Did they find my second pair of boots? My passport? My sunblock?''

Jack's face darkened with anger. ''I went through hell, Casey, and I don't like your flippant attitude about it.''

''I'm sorry,'' she said softly, relenting when she saw the pain on his face. ''It's just that the past week has been so crazy, and we've never had a chance to discuss everything.''

''Well, I saw Nan off on her flight and she'll be gone at least a week, so there's no reason why we can't take advantage of this time to talk now,'' he suggested. ''How about some dinner?''

Casey cocked her head to one side, watching Jack as if he was an interesting specimen she might have viewed through her microscope.

''I don't care to change my clothes,'' she said finally.

He studied her yellow shorts and tank top. ''I think I can find a place that will let you in.''

She hopped up. ''I'll put on some shoes.''

Jack thought of Nan, who would say something about freshening her lipstick, then end up taking more than an hour to get ready. Casey was back in a few minutes with sandals on her feet, a gleam of coral lipstick on her lips and her hair brushed back in casual disarray. She'd slipped a short-sleeved matching jacket on to protect her from the offshore breezes.

When they reached his car, she gave the dark green BMW a scathing look before sliding into the passenger seat.

"I would have thought you'd be driving a Mercedes," she commented.

"Try a truce for a while, all right?"

She shrugged. "All right, but I don't think it will be as much fun." She took her time adjusting her seat and the flow of air in her direction.

Jack had known immediately where he would take Casey. While Nan wasn't a snob, she did have her limits, and this particular restaurant hadn't proved to be one of her favorites, although Jack did enjoy going there and having the opportunity to just sit back and relax.

"So, did you decide if you're going over to the medical center for a look-see?" he asked, turning onto the highway that ran parallel to the ocean.

"I agreed to look over the facilities," she replied, slipping her sunglasses on. "Why?"

"I guess a high-profile position with a high-profile medical center would pay the bills for all those new clothes you're flaunting," he grumbled, tightly gripping the steering wheel. He was already tempted to put his hands around her throat.

"You know, it was amazing," she drawled. "When I got back, the institute immediately handed me a hefty check. They must have felt very guilty about what happened and the money made their guilt go away. That and because they were afraid I was going to sue them. It's a good thing they were so generous, since I discovered you had not only moved away, but naturally my checking account was closed. I didn't have so much as a driver's license, which wasn't all that easy to replace even though I was lucky enough to have a replacement passport with me to use as proof of my identity. When I got back I immediately got a copy of my birth certificate. I guess you wouldn't have it anymore, would you?" She shifted the seat back farther and unconcernedly stretched her legs up, propping her feet on the dashboard.

Jack swallowed the moan at the idea of his precious car being so cruelly mistreated. And, damn her, Casey knew exactly what she was doing. She knew he always treated his cars like a treasured possession that required hand-washing and hand-waxing on a weekly basis and careful cleaning of the interior.

He took a deep breath. "Does barbecue sound all right to you?" he asked.

Casey shrugged. "Anything is fine with me." She crossed one ankle over the other. "Do you like it out here, Jack?" She turned her head so she could see his face. "It's a faster pace than a small university town and definitely more upscale. Is that what you've always longed for?"

"I decided there had to be more to life than the classroom," he said quietly. "We lived inland, where the largest body of water was the university pool and our most important citizen was the dean and not the mayor. Here, it's difficult to say who's the most important because everyone thinks they're important. The ocean is in my backyard, I don't have to lecture to students who only take my class because they need the credit. I don't have to read and grade essays that would have been better written by a chimpanzee, and I don't have to kowtow to department heads. I feel as if out here I've been able to find the real me. And I've gotten to like the person I've become."

"You were the top choice to take over for Dr. Parrish when he retired," she said softly.

"I may have been top choice, but that didn't mean I wanted it."

Casey put her legs down and twisted in the seat. "You really are happier with yourself now, aren't you?" she commented.

"Sure, I didn't turn into an academic snob," he said, turning a hard right and pulling into a dirt parking lot.

Casey looked around with interest. What sat in front of her could only be described as a shack with most of it hanging over a cliff, looking as if it was ready to fall into the ocean at any moment. The ramshackle sign in front sported no lights and probably hadn't been painted in the past fifty years. Only one word was on the sign: Stoney's. She didn't bother waiting for Jack to come around to her side. She hopped out and looked around at the assortment of battered pickups and cars.

"I guess I wouldn't find this place in any of the city's dining guides, would I?" she commented.

"No one serves better barbecue," he told her, escorting her to the open front door that sagged on its hinges.

"Then, I guess they won't care if any of the sauce drips on the floor, will they?" Casey said.

She was pleasantly surprised when she entered and discovered the interior wasn't as decrepit as the exterior.

Tables were fashioned from telephone cable spools with chairs made from barrels. The music was loud country western from a jukebox, and a bar lined one entire wall. But what she noticed the most was the open-air balcony that overlooked the ocean and the rich aroma of meat cooked in spicy barbecue sauce. Her mouth immediately started salivating.

"Hey there, teach!" one man called out, lifting a beer mug in greeting. "You haven't been around in a while. Now I see why." He jokingly leered at Casey.

"Hank, how's it hanging?" Jack called back.

As he escorted Casey to the balcony, others called out to him, too.

"Something tells me you spend a lot of time here," she said as he seated her in one of the chairs.

"I did when I first arrived," he admitted. "Stoney's is the complete opposite of what I was used to. I could come in here and just be me."

Casey stared at him, stunned by what she was hearing. She opened her mouth to say something, but the waitress's arrival cut her short.

"Teach, good to see you," the woman greeted Jack with a casual ruffle of her fingers through his hair. She glanced at Casey curiously. "What can I get you?"

Jack looked to Casey.

"Do you have any Red Wolf?" she asked, naming a brand of beer and ignoring Jack's look of surprise.

"Same for me, Jodi," he muttered.

She nodded and walked off, her slender hips encased in short shorts that swung seductively with every step she took.

"I didn't think you drank beer," Jack commented.

"I developed a taste for it. The natives used to make this beer that was so potent a few sips could knock you on your butt," she told him. "After you've had that a few times, drinking regular beer is nothing more than drinking water." She picked up the menu that was jammed between the salt and pepper shakers. "Do you have any suggestions?"

"Everything they have here is good."

"Are you two ready to order?" Jodi deposited a bottle of beer in front of each of them.

Casey still studied the menu. "I'll have the beef ribs with the coleslaw and potato wedges along with a side of garlic bread."

"I'll take the same," Jack said when Jodi looked at him with an inquiring expression. "And could you bring me another beer with dinner?"

She nodded. "Sure thing."

Jack turned back to Casey, looking uncertain what to say next.

"We've taken a situation and turned it into a bigger mess than it started out to be," she said, apparently deciding to break the silence. "This may sound cruel, but Norton doesn't look as if he's knocking at death's door. In fact, he looks in excellent health for a man who thought he would be dying by the end of the year."

Jack shifted uncomfortably. "I told you. He had a heart attack and was told he had to stop working or risk another one. He was afraid if a family member didn't remain in charge, a rival would come in to take over. He talked to Nan and me for a long time about that." He looked pensive. "Then he talked to me privately. He asked me for my help. I couldn't do a lot for him, but marrying Nan was something I could do for him. I could give him peace of mind."

Casey looked away, because at that moment she couldn't bear to look at him.

"No wonder they say truth is stranger than fiction," she said finally. "Still, it's hard to believe you would be willing to enter a marriage of convenience.

That's like something out of a gothic novel. You saving the damsel so she won't lose her inheritance." She looked down, tracing an invisible path with her fingernail on the table. Then she looked up with a somber expression darkening her eyes. "None of this is right, Jack. Dan is chasing me around because he thinks I'm single. Nan thinks she's married to you when it really isn't valid, and it's turned out you and I aren't the same people we were three years ago."

Jack stiffened. "What are you trying to say, Casey? That you want a divorce?"

Her reply was delayed by the waitress's arrival with their meals.

Casey remained silent until Jodi left after being assured they didn't require anything else.

"Why don't we wait until we finish dinner before talking this out," she suggested. "I apologize. I shouldn't have even brought this up until then. I don't know about you, but I'd hate to ruin my appetite when this all looks so good." She picked up a sauce-drenched rib and brought it to her lips. She nibbled on the meat and then started delicately tearing the tender meat from the bone with her teeth. "You were right, this is great barbecue," she mumbled in between bites. She picked up a slice of garlic bread and bit into it.

Jack watched Casey eat with more gusto than he'd ever seen before. He always remembered her ladylike table manners, but this time she seemed oblivious to barbecue sauce coating her fingers and a slight smear on her cheek as she dug into her food.

And dammit, he found her uninhibited hunger arousing! An arousal that quickly left him when he remembered that she hinted that a divorce might be in their future.

He silently ordered his imagination to shut down so he could turn his attention to his own food, but his usual hunger for the spicy food was tempered by the woman seated across from him. He had brought her here to see how she would react to the blue-collar restaurant. Instead of showing disdain for the crude surroundings, she'd looked around with interest and happily applied herself to her meal.

He watched her look out over the water.

"Doesn't anyone worry about falling into the water if there's an earthquake while they're out here?" she asked in a hushed voice.

"The shack has been here since the late forties and no one's worried about it so far," he replied. "If it bothers you, we can move inside."

She shook her head. Strands of hair floated around her face due to the evening breeze. She used the back of her hand to push them away from her face.

"I guess if it hasn't fallen in fifty years, I shouldn't worry it might happen in the next five minutes." She picked up her beer bottle and drank thirstily. She glanced over toward the bar when loud voices intruded. She smiled at the sight of three men, all in their fifties, who were singing lustily and very out of tune.

"Something tells me they'll never make the finals in 'Star Search,'" she quipped with a grin.

"They don't mind. They're just in there enjoying themselves," he pointed out.

"That's what counts." Casey finished off the last rib and used the moist towelette to clean her hands.

Jack stared at her now bare plate. "You didn't leave a thing."

"I had a salad for lunch. I needed something more substantial." She picked up the menu. "Oh, good, cheesecake for dessert." She looked up when Jodi came over to take their plates.

"Dessert for anyone?" the waitress asked.

Casey nodded. "Your cheesecake and coffee please."

Jodi glanced at Jack.

"Just coffee for me. I think I'll just sit here and see if she can finish the cheesecake."

"Do not even assume I will share," Casey told him with a playful laugh. "I intend to eat every bite."

"You haven't seen the portion of cheesecake they give you."

Jack chuckled when Casey's eyes widened at the large wedge of dessert served to her, but she firmly informed him he wasn't getting one bite. She proved her statement by slowly eating her treat and not offering him a taste. He didn't mind. He'd already decided he would prefer the taste of cheesecake on her, anyway.

CASEY SIPPED HER COFFEE and allowed herself to enjoy the view. With the sun just setting, the water was a riot of brilliant blues, greens and oranges with the sun looking like a fireball on the horizon.

"I admit the view is nicer than at Lucky's Pizza Parlor," she commented, naming the popular student hangout in their former university town.

"It's also a lot warmer out here," he told her. "No snow during the winter. I don't have to scrape ice off the windows or shovel snow before I can back the car out of the garage. I don't have to wear four layers of clothing or be required to attend the football games."

"No faculty meetings," she joined in. "No studying a new batch of students and wondering how many would be left by the end of the year. No spending hours in the lab feeling as if I'm going blind while I look through a microscope."

Jack frowned at her last comment. "I thought you enjoyed research."

Casey shrugged. She picked up her cup and sipped more coffee. "I think I enjoyed it because I considered it safe. No one expected anything from me except results, and I could easily give them the results they wanted. There wasn't any challenge in it."

"Is that why you jumped at Greg's offer?" He

couldn't keep the bite out of his voice. "Because you didn't like research any longer?"

She set her cup down and pushed back her chair. "Why don't we take a walk?" she suggested. "I think I'll use the ladies' room right now."

While she was gone, Jack settled the bill and waited for her by the front door. He didn't say anything as they walked outside to the car.

"There's no easy way to get to the beach from here," he said, opening the passenger door.

He drove down the highway a ways until he reached a public parking lot. He pulled in and parked at the far end. Casey slipped off her sandals and left them in the car. She stepped onto the sun-warmed sand and immediately dug her toes down as deep as they'd go. When she realized Jack was watching her, she laughed self-consciously.

"It feels good," she explained.

When he held out his hand, she took it and followed him down to the water's edge.

"I think we've ignored the obvious long enough, Casey," he said crisply. "Do you want a divorce?"

Casey inwardly winced at the word. "To be honest, I don't know. Of course, I'm only speaking for myself. You might have other ideas on that subject. For now, I would think it would only make matters worse," she said quietly. "I know things weren't the best between us when I left, and I guess I thought our time apart would give us a chance to figure out what we wanted to do with our lives. I just didn't expect things to turn out the way they did.''

He didn't look down at her. ''No, I guess we didn't. What do you want, Casey?''

She remained quiet for a moment. ''I came back here thinking you and I could have a chance to see if we were meant to stay together. It appears, for now, that isn't possible. I would like to suggest something.''

''All right.''

Casey took a deep breath. She stopped and turned to face him. ''For now, I'll continue acting as your sister. I feel the need to get back to work, so I'll see if there's anything available in this area. That will give us a chance to get to know each other again and for you to consider your position with Nan and also with Norton. That way we'll have the chance to see if we want to make this marriage work. I do think you should tell Nan the truth about me as soon as possible. I don't want her to find out by accident or after the two of you part. At the same time, if you and Nan decide you want to remain married...'' Her voice drifted off for a moment, then returned stronger. ''If you do, then you would have to make arrangements for a second wedding ceremony.'' She resolutely kept her eyes on his, although she felt it was one of the hardest things she'd ever done.

''So if I decide I'd rather stay with Nan you'll give me a divorce without any problems?'' he asked.

She nodded jerkily. ''But I will be looking for my

own place in the next week or so. Living in your guest house is more than a little too strange for me.'' She turned around and started walking down the beach again.

"Wait a minute," he muttered, hurrying to catch up. He cocked his arm around her neck and pulled her head closer to his shoulder. "This doesn't mean you're going to date, does it?"

"None of your business. I'm single, remember?"

"But you're also my sister, and as your big brother I have an obligation to watch over you and make sure you don't get into any trouble."

"And as your sister, I will only tell you to back off."

"Meaning you're not going to date. You won't go out with someone if they ask you."

"Meaning it's none of your business."

"I told you. I'm only looking out for your best interests."

Casey mock-punched him in the stomach and walked away from him. When she was a few steps away, she turned around and walked backward.

"Do us both a favor, Jack. Don't look out for my best interests or you'll discover I know some very nasty ways of making you hurt," she threatened.

He threw up his hands. "A man asks a simple question...."

"Ha! It was not a simple question and you know it. If a good-looking man with charm and personality asks me out, it will be between him and me," she told him. "Which is exactly why I plan to find my own place."

She could have sworn she saw a flicker of pain cross his gaze before he masked it and seemed to mentally shore up his defenses.

"Fine, have it your way. But let me check him out first. Just to make sure he's not a serial killer."

Casey rolled her eyes at his crazy statement. "Right, all serial killers have their own listing, so you can find them easier. I mean it, Jack, don't push this any further or you'll be sorry." She spun around and walked away.

"Just for the record," he called out, "how sorry would I be?" He caught up with her, grabbed her shoulders and spun her around. "Casey, I've gotten you back after three years of hell. I don't want to think something could happen to you."

She didn't doubt his serious tone, but her smile wasn't the reassuring type.

"That's hard to think about when you have another wife to worry about," she said quietly, stepping out of his hold.

He reached for her and brought her back into his embrace. "What matters is you."

She started to shake her head then stopped. "Let's see if you can tell me that in a year, shall we?"

Chapter Eight

When Casey left the guest house to depart for the medical center, she noticed a white piece of paper slipped under her car's windshield wiper. She pulled it out and opened it to see Jack's bold scrawl.

Show 'em your stuff, babe.

"Babe? He called me babe?" she muttered, unlocking the car door and sliding inside. "Honestly, the man has lost all of his values. I dare him to call me that to my face."

As promised, Gerald was in the lobby to greet her when she arrived.

At first glance, Casey saw a reception area decorated in warm pastels and soft classical music playing softly from hidden speakers. The patients waiting were mostly female, all well dressed.

"I thought your sign indicated you have pediatricians here," she commented, noting the lack of anyone under the age of twelve.

"We have two special waiting areas for the children," he explained, guiding her down a hallway.

"One for well children and another for those who are infectious. Nurse's aides look after them so they're well taken care of." He indicated the two rooms decorated in bold primary colors.

Gerald missed nothing as he took the next two hours to show Casey the state-of-the-art laboratories, outpatient operating rooms and examination rooms.

"We can handle pretty much any emergency here that a hospital can," he explained, as he pointed out several of the doctors' private offices and led the way to his own. "We can also have a helicopter from the hospital here in five minutes for trauma cases." He opened the door to his office and ushered her inside.

Casey's eyes almost bugged out at the opulence before her.

"The sight of a successful doctor's office tells the patients they'll be well cared for," Gerald explained when he noticed her expression. "We take care of many important people, including several ex-senators, a few congressmen, heads of international corporations and film stars. They know when they come to us they're getting the best care possible."

The best care money can buy was what came to her mind as she seated herself in a plush chair placed next to a coffee table set up with an elaborate silver coffee service. She made sure none of her thoughts could be read on her face and only a bland smile showed.

Gerald poured coffee and handed her a delicate china cup. "Of course, we also do a lot of good here," he went on. "If someone without insurance comes in, we will do what we can and send them on to the proper facility."

Casey nodded. "That is admirable, sir."

He smiled, obviously not detecting the hint of sarcasm in her voice. "We do our best for those who can't afford medical care. Now—" he clapped his hands together "—what do you say to joining us? I've checked your credentials, and I must say you have an impressive background in research and academics but little of hands-on other than those years working in the jungle." His face twisted just a bit with disdain. "You were extremely lucky you didn't come home with a nasty virus or parasite."

"I'm a product of healthy living," she said, sipping her coffee. If nothing else, she would work here just for the coffee.

"After looking over your credentials, we had a meeting and knew you would fit in here nicely. Not to mention, give us a little more prestige," he smirked. "I'm sure you'll be publishing a paper on your experiences down there."

Casey paused. "The way you've discussed the center's setup, it sounds more like a law office with the partners, associates and on down the line."

He nodded. "We do carefully screen our people. We want only the cream of the crop practicing here. Naturally, we make it more than worthwhile." He named a salary that almost had her sliding off her chair in shock. "Along with that are stock options, a generous pension, a car and more than enough time for you to attend any medical seminars you feel would be beneficial.''

She smiled, sensing he felt he'd snared her in. She wanted to tell him she'd learned that money and prestige weren't everything and publishing a paper on her experiences didn't mean what it used to.

''I have to say you do know how to treat a girl,'' she murmured with a just hint of coy shyness in her voice. ''You won't mind if I have some questions of my own, will you?''

He sat back, convinced she was one hooked fish. ''Of course not.''

''How many patients do you treat in a week who truly need medical attention other than you holding their hand and perhaps prescribing a placebo just to keep them happy?''

Gerald sat forward. His face darkened as he stared back at her. For a moment, she swore he was ready to pull off that expensive silk tie and strangle her with it.

''We practice medicine here, Dr. Larson,'' he said coldly.

''I would just like to know,'' she said quickly, as if backpedaling. ''After all, I've seen some impressive medical facilities where doctors don't take the time to truly get to know their patients, and I had to know you weren't like that.''

He immediately relaxed. ''I can see we'll have you to keep us on our toes.''

Casey left the center a half hour later with a set of unsigned contracts in her purse. She'd asked for time to look them over and for her attorney to check them out. Gerald assured her she would be welcome as soon as she signed them, and even went so far as to show her the office she would be occupying. She couldn't argue with the fourth-floor view of the beach. She wondered out loud how she would be able to concentrate with such a lovely view, but Gerald assured her they had all felt that way but soon learned to ignore it.

Not caring to return to the house just yet, she decided to leave her car in the parking lot and wander through the nearby shopping area.

"Perfect, see your doctor then go shopping to recover from all the poking and prodding," she murmured, walking down the sidewalk and stopping in front of an art gallery to study the paintings in the display window. After deciding there was nothing there that held her interest, she went on, pausing at some windows and going in some shops, when she saw something that caught her eye.

Casey had always enjoyed her work, but she admitted to herself that this free time was a nice bonus. She had been given the opportunity to decide what she wanted to do with her life. Although, this free time also held the frustration of dealing with Jack.

"Good thing no one around here knows me," she muttered to herself. "Or we'd both be in big trouble."

After stopping for a quick lunch, Casey decided to

take her purchases and return to her car. She knew she would have to look over the contract and determine if working with Gerald's elite group was what she wanted to do. The sooner she did it, the sooner she would come to a decision one way or the other.

"Hey, jungle queen!"

Casey spun around at the sound of the ridiculous title sung out by a male voice. The man walking toward her wore a broad grin and outstretched arms.

"Greg?" She wasn't sure whether to believe her eyes or not.

"One and the same." He gathered her up in his arms and spun her around. "My God, you look great." He set her down and stood back, even though he kept his hands on her arms. "It's amazing what a haircut and new clothes do for a person. What are you doing out here?"

He can't know the truth.

"For one, I'm thinking about opening a practice out here," she replied, figuring a half lie wasn't bad.

He arched an eyebrow. "You're kidding. I'll be honest, I can't see Jonathon out here. There's no staid academic life around here that I know of."

"Actually, he's been living out here for a couple years now," she said. "He felt it was time for a change and I think he's right. What about you?"

He grinned self-consciously. "Have time for some lunch so we can catch up?"

"I just finished lunch, but I'm willing to have some coffee."

They entered a small café and were seated.

Casey set her packages on the floor and looked at him inquiringly.

"All right, you win," he chuckled, holding up his hands. "But I have a pretty good idea you aren't going to believe what I'm going to tell you."

"I love a good story."

Casey couldn't believe the Greg she was seeing. If she didn't know any better, she'd swear he seemed uncertain.

"I'm helping run a free clinic," he admitted.

Casey stared at him. At the moment, she couldn't think of a single thing to say.

"A free clinic?" she repeated.

He nodded. "I know. The Greg you knew wouldn't have set foot inside a clinic that didn't cater to the wealthy, but I went through a lot of internal revelations after we got back."

"I think we both did," Casey replied.

Greg looked her over and grinned. "It seems your changes were more external, while mine were more internal."

"Oh, mine were internal, too, believe me."

"What does Jonathon think of the new you?" he asked.

Casey grinned back. "He was stunned." She was pleased she didn't have to lie about that. "But then Jonathon's changed, too. He prefers to be called Jack now and he's no longer teaching."

"It must be quite an adjustment for both of you after all this time," he commented.

You have no idea. Casey's smile didn't waver. "Maybe more than usual, since we both have changed so much. In fact, I have to say you've changed, too. So far, you haven't tried to grope me once."

Greg's face turned a bright red. "I'd like to apologize for the hell I must have given you."

"Only until I set you straight," she said primly.

He winced. "A black eye does tell a man not to try something again." He paused when the waitress approached them and took their orders.

"So tell me why you're working in a free clinic," she prodded.

"After we got back, I felt at loose ends. I had no desire to stay with the institute, and luckily a friend had asked me to come out to see him. I didn't waste any time in flying out to San Diego. That was when I learned Ron was running the clinic. He was understaffed, always seemed to need something, was overrun with patients all the time—and he couldn't be happier. I ended up helping him out for a few days and discovered it was just what I needed to do."

Casey looked skeptical at his words. "No offense, Greg, but this doesn't sound like you at all."

"I'd be the first to admit I couldn't see me doing it, either," he said with a rueful smile, "but as crazy as it sounds, my soul-searching showed me a new side to myself, and I found out this new side is a hell of a lot easier to live with."

Casey eyed him, unsure whether he was trying a new scam or telling the truth. "Does this mean you're paying for my coffee?"

"Yes, I'm paying for your coffee." He chuckled.

She smiled at the waitress as the cup was set in front of her.

"You should come by," Greg told Casey, playfully slapping her hand as she stole one of his French fries.

"To see you actually working, I'd even pay admission," she teased.

"Don't worry, I won't charge you."

Casey leaned back in her chair, studying him, remembering the man she had dealt with in the jungle and the man who sat before her now. She couldn't see any of the arrogance of the man who thought he was God's gift to women. Come to think of it, he had been respectful to the waitress without being a boor as he usually was when a pretty woman was in the vicinity. Could it be possible he had changed? She didn't want to believe it, but the man sitting there wasn't at all like the man she knew.

"What on earth happened to you?"

He shrugged, looking even a little sheepish, as if he didn't want to go into great detail. "I grew up," he said simply. "Being down there, working with people who savored the world around them, was a teaching experience that showed me more than any seat of higher learning could have taught me."

"You have grown up," she murmured, with a trace of a smile. "Isn't it amazing that we both came back changed people?"

"It's also amazing we both ended up pretty much in the same place."

She grew a little wary of his comment, waiting for that inevitable come-on. Could this all be some elaborate scam he'd thought up? Was he going to hit on her next? Perhaps giving him that black eye wasn't enough. But no, Greg still sat there smiling and eating his lunch.

"How has it been with you and Jonathon—sorry, Jack—adjusting to each other's new self?" he asked. "After three years it must be difficult."

"It hasn't been easy," she admitted. "But we're doing a lot of talking, finding our way again."

"Maybe things will be even better for the two of you, then."

Casey could only hope he was right.

After Greg settled the bill, they walked outside together.

"Come down and see us," he urged again once they stopped by his car.

The first thing Casey noticed was that his car wasn't a sleek sporty model that the man usually favored, but a small pickup. She raised a questioning eyebrow.

"It's perfect for hauling supplies," he explained. He reached into his back pocket and pulled out a notepad, quickly sketching a map and directions. He handed her the piece of paper.

"It's really good to see you again, Casey." There was none of the leering male interest she remembered from before. "I'm glad we got this chance to get together."

She reached out and hugged him. "Thanks for the coffee. I'll make sure to come by."

As Casey drove back to the house, she replayed her conversation with Greg in her mind. She still had trouble believing the man she just saw was the same whiny pain in the butt she'd put up with for almost three years. Then she thought about Gerald, with his immaculately manicured hands, a surgeon's hands, which did little more than lift a scalpel. True, that's what he'd trained many years for, but did she know how many people he actually helped? Seeing people seated in the waiting room who didn't look as if they were even remotely ill bothered her. She had discovered she enjoyed healing. She wasn't sure she could go back to such a sterile environment, where colleagues would probably not agree with some of the holistic methods she'd learned the past few years.

"Maybe I'm not giving him the benefit of the doubt," she said out loud. "Just because people look healthy doesn't mean they are. You've said that enough times, Casey. Don't discount them just because they prefer going to a fancy clinic with equipment straight out of a science fiction movie to one that's basically limping along with what it can." She

slowed down and turned into the lane leading up to
Nan's house. She refused to consider it Nan and
Jack's house. Nan had been kind enough to give her
a garage door opener so she could keep her car pro-
tected. At a glance, she could see Jack hadn't returned
yet, but as it was barely three o'clock, she wasn't
surprised.

Casey pulled a bottle of sparkling mineral water
out of the refrigerator and filled a glass with ice. With
that and a small bowl of pretzels, she settled back on
the couch reading the thick contract. She muttered a
curse, pulled out her reading glasses and slipped them
on to better read the fine print.

"I don't know why attorneys like to draw up contracts using small print," she muttered, making notes
on a pad propped up against her bent knees.

She was slowly but steadily making her way
through the second page when a knock on the door
disturbed her concentration.

"Rats!" She put the papers to one side, got up and
opened the door. "What do you want?" she asked
Jack.

He loosened his tie, pulling the knot halfway down
and undoing the two top shirt buttons.

"Just wondering how your meeting over at Oceanview went." He walked in.

"Gerald offered me a position if I'm interested."
She walked back over to the couch and plopped back
down. She picked up the contract and her notepad.
"I'm making notes of questions I have. Gerald figures

my taking this contract meant I'd accept it. I told him that wasn't so. I figure my options are still open."

Jack held out his hand. "May I?"

She handed him the contract. She couldn't resist smiling at the way he squinted as he first held the paper close to his face, then held it at arm's length.

"You might have better luck with these," she suggested, handing him her reading glasses. As he sat down on the couch, she stood behind him, absently massaging his shoulders the way she used to when he'd come back from departmental meetings. "Honestly, Jack, you're so tense, your blood pressure must have jumped a good ten points. Take a few deep breaths."

"Deep-breathing exercises won't let me read without glasses. I used to have perfect eyesight," he grumbled, scanning the pages. In the same unconscious manner, he leaned back under her strong touch. "Now everything blurs unless I hold it a mile away. I can't believe they want you to sign this. Why don't they just ask you for all your blood and be done with it?" He slapped the sheaf of papers. "They want to tie you all up and turn you into a copy of them. The center is well thought of, but I can't believe they all signed a contract like this."

"Next you'll say he's doing wild medical experiments in the basement with monkey blood or something," she teased, digging her fingers into the tight muscles in his shoulders.

"Afraid you'll only see that in medical thrillers,

sweetheart. Gerald likes the idea of being top doc in this area. He likes to think he's got the power to play with all the big boys. I heard he started his medical practice here around the same time as Norton started up, and the two met and soon became good friends. They each have their own form of power games they enjoy playing.''

''To each his own,'' she said airily. ''Just put the paper down, Jack, and stop blowing steam out of your ears.'' She began massaging his scalp.

Jack immediately relaxed under her tender ministrations. He groaned with pleasure as her fingers seemed to find the right pressure points.

''How does that feel?'' she whispered in his ear.

''Don't stop,'' he moaned, his entire body seeming to move with the slow, languorous movement of her fingers. He closed his eyes and lifted his hands to gently circle her wrists with his fingers as if to ensure she wouldn't stop. ''Remember that old claw-foot tub we had?'' he murmured.

''Big enough and deep enough to swim in,'' Casey said softly, her hands lingering on his shoulders and moving downward of their own accord.

If Jack didn't know better he would have sworn he had imbibed a few too many beers. His head was swimming, and the world seemed to dip and sway in front of him. Not to mention the heady aroma of her perfume spinning an intriguing spell inside his head.

''I don't remember our ever trying to swim in it,'' he mumbled.

"Oh, yes, we did," she murmured, her lips still close to his ear. "It was our first night in the house. We used too much bubble bath and the tub overflowed, remember?"

His hazy brain brought up the details with graphic clarity. "Oh, yeah."

"And you got out of the tub, slipped in the water and fell on your butt, and when you tried to help me out of the tub, I slipped against you and we both fell down," she said against his ear. "And we decided we may as well stay there."

Jack felt as if all the breath had been sucked out of his lungs. He was positive that any moment he would turn into a puddle of sensation and slide right down to the carpet. Casey's fingers danced across his bare nape, sending shivers along his spine.

When her hands left his back he felt as if he had been abandoned. For a moment, he was tempted to turn around and pull her down onto his lap. He settled for looking over his shoulder.

"Thank you for the shoulder rub," he said formally.

Her lips danced with a smile as if she knew just how informal his thoughts were. "My pleasure."

He coughed to clear his throat. "What would you say to getting something to eat?"

"I'm not in any mood to go out. If you don't mind something simple, I can scramble some eggs or heat up some chili," she offered.

"Either is fine with me." Jack stood up, disconcerted to find his legs a bit wobbly. "I'll even help."

"Not if you still cook as badly as before. You can get out dishes and silverware. We'll rough it and eat at the coffee table." She dug a frying pan out of the cabinet under the stove. "Why don't you put some bread in the toaster, too?"

"Do you still like yours barely toasted?"

"Is there any other way? Certainly not the charcoal shade you prefer," Casey teased, breaking eggs into a bowl and adding a little milk.

"When you were in the jungle, did you find yourself missing certain foods?" he asked as he gathered up plates and silverware.

"Did I?" she laughed. "Most definitely chocolate. There were times I would have killed for chocolate. I remember I'd lie there visualizing my favorite chocolate candy and wanting to scream because there wasn't any way I could jump in a car and go out and get some."

"And?"

She looked up, thinking for a moment. "Chocolate mint ice cream. Butter-toffee peanuts. Milk Duds. Pizza. Chinese food. Some nights I swore I was getting heartburn just thinking about all of it. And I didn't have any Alka-Seltzer to even take care of imaginary upset stomachs." She chuckled. "I even missed the daffodils we had in the backyard."

"What did you do when you first got back?" he asked.

"Easy. I bought five pounds of my favorite candy and sat down and promptly ate it all. I was so sick afterward it wasn't funny."

Jack winced. "I would think that would cure you of chocolate."

Casey shook her head. "Are you kidding? I just reminded myself I didn't have to eat it all at once," she said with a smirk. "Now I limit myself to one or two pieces a day."

"No craving for steak, lobster, French toast?"

"Not really." She grated cheddar cheese in the eggs. "I was eating a variety of new foods that made up for it a little."

"Such as?" He held the plates while she spooned out scrambled eggs and buttered toast.

"There were these grubs that were very fat and white and were pretty tasty after they had been cooked. I pretended they were shrimp," she explained, pouring wine into two glasses and carrying them into the tiny living room. "They caught fish that weren't too bad. Naturally, roots and berries. And they considered some of the snakes a delicacy." She wrinkled her nose. "It took some time to get accustomed to the new tastes. Come to think of it, I also missed coffee and Coke. I was lucky I didn't catch anything drinking the water."

Jack picked up his wineglass and toasted her. "You were one brave lady."

Her smile dimmed. "No, I wasn't. Pardon the cliché, but I had to make the best of a bad situation.

Learning to eat worms was just a part of it.'' She forked up some egg and brought it to her lips.

Jack looked down at his eggs. "I guess I shouldn't have brought up your culinary habits before we ate," he muttered.

"I guess it's a good thing I didn't cook shrimp."

Jack groaned but gamely ate his food.

"What else did you do today?"

"Oh, girl stuff," she quipped, sipping her wine. "Shopping."

He shook his head in amazement. "You don't like shopping."

"I've discovered it can be fun. Especially since I don't need to dress like the head matron in a prison movie." She absently ran her fingers through her hair, which immediately fluffed around her face.

Jack looked at her bronze-colored hair and copper earrings dangling in multisize triangles. She looked delicious in her cream-colored tank top and long patchwork skirt. A faint scent of something floral drifted off her skin.

"You never wore that type of perfume before," he murmured.

She twitched her nose. "You never wore anything stronger than aftershave, and now you seem to go for something with a bit more punch," she replied.

"A lot of men wear cologne," Jack countered.

"I'm not complaining. It's actually very nice." She leaned forward and sniffed his neck. "A bit of spice, a bit of citrus, nothing floral. Very you."

"Thank you so much," he said dryly. "I had no idea I'd need your approval for whatever cologne I wear."

"Maybe not, but I approve, anyway. I have to say you've turned so spiffy in the past few years. Classy threads." She fingered his shirt collar. "Professionally styled hair, cologne. I'm just surprised you haven't taken up surfing."

"I tried it and almost drowned. That's when I decided to settle for bodysurfing," he said. "Besides, you're not exactly the same, either. Short hair—" he fingered the wispy strands "—shorter clothes—" he allowed his gaze to linger on her bare legs where her skirt had hiked up "—and a sassy attitude."

"Sassy attitude?" she teased.

He nodded. "When I saw you at the wedding, I thought for sure I was seeing a ghost. I couldn't believe it was you, especially the way you were dressed." He drew imaginary circles in the eggs with his fork.

Casey's mouth twisted in a wry smile. "I assume I didn't look at all like the woman you married. Besides, you looked pretty snazzy in that tuxedo."

"Yes, I saw the woman I married," he corrected her. "But I also saw the vision she had become. Someone who could twist any man into knots with little trouble. I couldn't miss the way other men looked at you as if you were a decadent dessert they couldn't wait to devour."

"Mmm, dessert," she murmured, rolling her

tongue around her fork. "You make me sound sinful."

"That, too." His voice grew husky. He stared at her as if she was, indeed, a sinful dessert he wouldn't mind devouring himself.

Casey's eyes gleamed as she watched him. "Such as?" Her voice caressed him like hot silk.

"Warm caramel over ice cream. Rich and creamy, a taste that invites more."

She slowly lifted a forkful of egg to her mouth. "One taste isn't enough?"

"Never," he murmured.

Casey's gaze never left his as she slowly chewed her food. "I was raised that you had to finish your dinner before you could consider dessert."

Jack chuckled at her comment, which effectively dispelled the growing tension between them. He knew this attraction was wrong. The timing was wrong. But that knowledge didn't help. Not when he could look at her and want her more than he ever had.

"I wonder what would have happened if you had come home when you were scheduled to," he mused aloud.

Casey shrugged. "You would have still been lobbying for the philosophy chair and I would have returned to my teaching and we might have decided that we couldn't remain together any longer," she murmured, not looking up at him. "We would have drifted apart without bothering to find out what went wrong."

"Maybe if we'd had children..." He stared into his wineglass, as if all the answers could be found in its contents.

Her laughter held no humor, and her gaze was bleak with sorrowful memories. "Oh, Jack, we would have been the worst parents that could be found. Any child in his right mind would leave us the day he was born," she said cynically. "The star in the philosophy department and the star in medicine couldn't handle their own lives, much less guide someone else's. We were better off not having children and exposing them to our foibles."

"Maybe kids would have brought us back to the real world sooner," Jack said softly. He drew up one leg and rested his arm on his knee. His half-filled wineglass dangled between his fingers. He brought the glass to his lips and drank the tart liquid. "We would have had someone else to worry about."

"You don't have children to save a marriage, Jack. You have them to enrich what you already have." She picked at the remainder of her dinner and then looked off in the distance. "I don't want to talk about this anymore."

Jack expected the silence between them to be wrought with tension. Instead, it was strangely peaceful. Without saying a word, he put his glass on the coffee table, picked up the plates and carried them into the kitchen. He brought back the wine bottle and topped off both glasses. Then he turned on the radio and soft music drifted across the room, lending to the relaxed atmosphere.

He walked back to Casey and held his hand out. Her face was expressionless as she placed her hand in his and allowed him to pull her to her feet. When he folded his arms around her, she automatically tensed.

"It's just a dance, Casey," he murmured, leading her in the slow, intricate steps.

Her hand was cool inside his, her other hand perched lightly on his shoulder. Their legs occasionally brushed as they moved to the love song. At first, she had her head tipped back so she could watch him, but after a while, she rested her cheek against his chest. The soft scent of her hair drifted up to his nostrils, the silky strands lying brightly against his shirt. He was positive he could hear the sound of her heartbeat echo in his mind, the beat growing unsteadier with each pulse, just as his own faltered. He silently willed her to look at him again. He wanted to see what was in her eyes. He always believed he knew what she was thinking if he could look into her eyes.

As if she heard his unspoken request, she tipped her head back and looked directly into his face. This time her gaze was unreadable. It was as if she wore a mask. But still, there was something there—a flame within the dark depths—that gave him pause.

His head dipped just a bit; hers lifted just a bit. Her breath was warm on his skin. Her lips were so close to his that Jack could almost feel her kiss. Closing his eyes, he leaned into her, ready to claim the kiss he'd waited for for three years....

"I think you should go."

Was he hearing things? Surely that wasn't Casey's quiet voice telling him to go home. Not now. But then, as if to confirm, she stiffened in his arms.

Jack thought about arguing with her. He thought about reminding her they still had things to discuss. He wanted to finish this dance. There was so much he wanted that he wasn't sure where to begin. But dammit, he'd say anything as long as he could keep her in his arms.

She was the one to break contact by stepping back. His arms dropped.

Jack had no choice.

"Thank you for dinner," he murmured, before he let himself out.

If he had looked back, he would have seen Casey sink down to the floor and drop her forehead to her knees.

She remained in that position for a long time.

JACK STOOD at his bedroom window staring at the guest house. He noticed the living room light was still on despite the late hour.

What should he have done? What should he have said? The question had sounded in his mind all night.

The soft tone of his phone ringing slowly brought him back to the present. He picked up the cordless phone on the bedside table.

"Yes?"

"Did I wake you?" It was Nan.

He sat down on the edge of the bed. "Naw. In fact, the strippers just left with the police. I was told it was some hot party until the cops showed up."

"That's right, have fun when I'm not around," Nan mock-groused.

"How's it going back there?"

"Better than I thought. They're actually listening to me. I did what you suggested and put myself in my father's shoes and stayed toe-to-toe with them on every one of their arguments. With luck, we'll have this wrapped up in a week."

"That's great. I'm glad it's going well." He settled back with his pillows plumped up behind him.

For the next ten minutes, they traded stories of their day's activities. As Jack listened to Nan, he realized that while he could feel affection for her, there was none of the intensity he felt for Casey. Right now would have been an excellent time to tell her about Casey, but he knew he couldn't do it over the phone.

"Jack, are you there?" Nan's voice sounded in his ear.

"Sorry. What was that you said?"

"Only that it's even later here and I need to get some sleep. Jack?" She waited for him to reply. "I really do thank you for all the support you've given me on this."

"You could have done this on your own, Nan, if you'd been willing to make the fight."

"Yes, but with Daddy's fragile health, I didn't want to take any chances. Thank you again," she murmured. "Good night, darling."

"Good night, Nan." Jack disconnected and lay back. But instead of wondering what Nan was doing, his mind had immediately wandered in Casey's direction.

"SO, HOW'S HUBBY?"

Nan turned around to face the man lounging on the other half of the bed. He had recently taken a shower and his towel was slipping farther down by the moment. There was no denying what was on his mind.

"He's fine." She leaned over and traced his lips with her fingertips. "I hate to betray him this way."

He pulled her into his arms. "Since we both know the last person your father would want in your life is me, we had no choice." He nuzzled her throat. "Don't worry about him. Think about me."

Nan threw her head back, moaning as his fingers found her nipple.

"All I can say is I'm so glad you're not really my cousin."

Chapter Nine

Casey could tell by the state of the buildings that she was getting closer to the clinic. She'd driven inland, where the large stately homes slowly disappeared and strip malls and small businesses started to crop up. The homes were smaller and closer together, the people on the streets not as well dressed.

The sign over the clinic stated its business in three languages. When she'd parked and stepped into the building, she was assailed by the number of voices shouting and crying. There were so many people waiting. She looked around and found a table marked Reception. The girl seated behind it looked up with a smile but a wary curiosity in her gaze.

"Yes?" she asked, with a slight accent.

"I'm Dr. Larson. Dr. Matthews asked me to stop by," she explained.

The girl's dark eyes lit up with interest. "Oh, yes, I'll tell him you're here." She popped out of her chair and walked swiftly down the hall. Two minutes later, Greg strode toward her. Dressed in jeans and a

T-shirt, he didn't look like any doctor she'd seen before. His dark hair was mussed and his jaw shaded with a beard he probably hadn't had time to shave off that morning.

"Have you come to work?" He grinned, hugging her.

Casey stepped back and scanned him with a narrow gaze. "Is this the Greg Matthews who was appalled to discover the jungle was also used as a bathroom by the local residents?"

He shrugged. "What can I say? Come on back." He placed his hand against the small of her back as they walked down the hallway. "As you can see, we have five examination rooms." He gestured toward one room whose door was open.

Casey nodded. "What type of cases seem to be predominant here?"

"Malnutrition is a big one, along with infectious diseases. We also hold immunization clinics once a month," he explained.

At the end of the hall was an office that was more functional than decorative. A battered leather couch was pushed up against one wall, and a metal desk was set against another wall where a man was seated busily writing in a file. He looked up.

"Casey, this is Ron Willis," Greg said as they entered. "And Ron, this is Casey Larson. I'm hoping to talk her into joining us here."

"Yeah, Greg told me about running into you yesterday." He grinned at her. "So what do you think of our setup? I know it's not Oceanview, but we can offer you crazy hours and all the bad coffee you can drink. Not to mention some pretty incredible challenges.''

Greg showed Casey to a chair and perched on a corner of the desk. ''I'll be the first to admit a female doctor would be helpful at times.''

''And here I thought you wanted me for my medical skills,'' she teased.

Ron's grin sobered. ''I've been here for five years, and while the money isn't great, the rewards are. Our hours are long and working weekends is nothing new to us.''

Casey thought about the many people out front, all patiently waiting their turn for help. There wasn't any muted classical music coming from artfully hidden speakers or tasteful artwork to make the room more pleasant. She couldn't recall even seeing any magazines out there. She thought about the perks Gerald was offering her and the lovely office with a view of the ocean. The prestige of treating the socially and politically active.

She rested her fingers together steeple fashion. ''If there's one thing I can't stand, it's bad coffee, so I'll be in charge of that when I'm here. And—'' she held up a finger for emphasis ''— don't think you can fob off all the scut work on me, because I've learned some nasty tricks over the years and I won't hesitate to use them. Understood?'' She looked from Greg to Ron.

The two men stared at her as if they couldn't believe what they were hearing. Then they looked at each other in silent communication.

"You don't want to think it over?" Greg asked cautiously.

"Why? Is there anything else you want to warn me about?" she asked lightly. "I'm just relieved to know I won't have to learn to play golf." She took a quick look around. "I hope you won't mind if I bring a few things in to brighten up the place?"

"Anything as long as it isn't modern art," Ron said, grinning from ear to ear. "Picasso isn't our style here."

"I don't think you even have a style here." Casey stood up. "When would you like me to start?"

"Now would be great, but we'd settle for tomorrow," Greg said, sharing a look with his partner.

"Give me two days," she said.

There were no written contracts, no formal presentations. Just a handshake between the three of them.

"How will Jonathon feel about you working here?" Greg asked as he walked Casey out to her car. "I remember he wasn't all that happy about you going down to South America with me."

"Jack has changed in many ways," she said airily. "No, he won't mind. He was surprised I considered returning to active practice, so I know he won't mind at all."

Greg didn't look convinced.

"It's not what I planned, either," he admitted, looking at the graffiti-scarred building. "But I found peace here, so who am I to argue with fate?"

Casey leaned against the car door with her arms crossed in front of her chest. "It seems we've all taken a turn we didn't expect," she murmured. She smiled and reached out to hug him. "See you in two days." She unlocked her door and climbed in.

As she drove away, she realized she felt better than she had in some time. Her smile that had blossomed as she sped up the highway suddenly dimmed.

"Now all I have to do is figure out how I'm going to tell Jack about this."

"YOU WHAT?"

Casey winced at Jack's shout. "Aren't you happy I took a position that's for a good cause?"

"Are you sure you didn't take the position because good old *Greg* is there?" he asked in a snide voice.

She threw up her hands. "I get offered a plush corner office with an ocean view, a Mercedes and a stock option plan to rival most corporations," she said with dramatic flair. "But, because of a man's baby blues, I give it all up so I could work long hours in a tiny walk-in clinic. How astute you are, Dr. Larson. Any woman would be more than willing to make such a sacrifice for a man."

Jack sat there with his arms crossed in front of his chest and a pout on his face. "So you noticed the color of his eyes," he commented with a sneer.

Casey threw her hands up in disgust. "You are hopeless!"

"I'm not the one deciding to work with a guy I'd been marooned with for three years," he pointed out with a curled lip.

"I can hardly call it marooned when we were with about eighty people," she said, ice forming on each word.

"Ah." He held up his forefinger as he made his point. "But they probably believed the two of you were a couple."

Casey leaned forward. The fire in her eyes warned him that he was about to go up in flames. "Jack Larson, if you say one more word, you will lose complete use of your vocal chords. Do I make myself understood?"

He didn't deign to reply as he sulked. Instead, he stretched his legs out in front of him and lifted his face to the cooling evening breeze. Surely Casey hadn't expected him to take her news with good grace. Good grace? The last thing he wanted to hear was that Greg was living thirty miles south of here. And for a man who believed medicine was purely a prestige profession, why was he working with those who couldn't afford adequate medical care?

"How do you know Greg isn't just setting up some elaborate scam to get you back?" He wasn't about to let her have the last word.

Casey took a deep breath. "Greg can't plan something to get me back since he never had me."

Jack stared at the pool beyond them. "He was devious enough to get you to go to South America with him, so why shouldn't he try again?"

She turned in the chair, curving her legs over the arm. "Be careful, Jack, or I might think you're jealous," she taunted.

"I'm not jealous," he muttered in a sullen tone. "Just cautious." He laced his fingers over his flat belly.

Casey sat up. The grin on her face broadened by the second as she watched the red blooming his cheeks. "Yes, you are," she said gleefully. "Your face is practically green."

He glared at her. "I'm sure it has more to do with the company than anything else."

"I don't know what you have to be jealous about. I'm not the one with two wives."

"If you had two wives, people would definitely wonder."

Casey slouched back down. "I never thought green was your color, but I can see this one looks good on you. I'm just not sure whether to call it celery or pea green. No, more celadon, I think."

Jack looked at her as if he could cheerfully strangle her. He took several deep breaths as if he was trying to contain his temper.

"So, this clinic does a little of everything," he said, obviously having regained his composure but still not about to give up.

She nodded and went on to explain its operation.

"Admittedly, the equipment isn't up-to-date and they're constantly looking for funding, but they're doing good where they are. They're helping people."

"This just isn't you," he said candidly. "While I know you didn't go into medicine for the money, you didn't do it for the common man, either."

"I'm no longer that person," she argued, waving her hands for emphasis.

"No kidding," he muttered. "I don't see what's wrong with you working at Oceanview. You'd be dealing with people there, too," he pointed out.

"But those people don't need *me*," Casey said emphatically. "The patients I saw today do." She took a deep breath and squared her shoulders.. "This is what I intend to do, Jack."

"Good old Greg sure knew how to push your buttons, didn't he?"

Casey advanced on him. "I swear, Jack, if you say one more word about Greg, I will turn you into mush!" She began pounding on his shoulders with blows that weren't exactly harmless.

Jack tried to fend off her blows with little success. In the end, he snaked his arms around her waist and pulled her down onto his lap, effectively holding her arms at her side.

"Now, this isn't so bad." He laughed as she tried to wriggle out of his hold. He tightened his grip around her waist. "What do you want to do next? Wrestle?"

"You're only doing this because I was winning,"

she declared, keeping her hands on his shoulders for balance.

Jack reared back as her face grew closer to his. Her smile widened with just a hint of teeth showing.

"Afraid I'll bite, Jack?" she purred.

"No," he said cautiously as if his answer was actually the opposite.

"Don't worry, Jack, I won't bite," she assured him in that same purring voice as she looked at him under seductively lowered lids. "Unless you want me to."

Jack was positive he was looking at the original Eve tempting him as no other woman could. The sensual scent of her perfume wove another spell around him.

"Is that what you want, Jack?" Her voice was nothing more than a breathy whisper against his cheek. "Do you want me to nibble on you?" Her teeth grazed his neck.

He found his thought processes rapidly shutting down. For the life of him he couldn't come up with one coherent thought as he felt the silky texture of Casey's hair brush against his cheek and the cool satin of her fingertips against his skin. The luxurious feel of her breasts against his chest was another sensation he wasn't sure he could handle. He took a gulp of much-needed air. He immediately needed another when he looked into her eyes.

They were soft and luminous, warm as she gazed at him.

"How interesting," she murmured, trailing her fingertips across his shoulders. "You don't seem to mind my sitting here." She wiggled around until she obviously found a comfortable position.

The wiggling didn't do Jack's peace of mind any good. At that moment, he wanted nothing more than to rip her shirt off and see if he could find any tan lines. He wanted to cup her breast without the impediment of her clothing, and he doubted she would put up much of a fuss. It had been so long since he'd made love to his wife, his aroused mind reminded him as his fingers tiptoed their way up her spine, pressing her closer to him. Her lips were a glossy coral color, moist and slightly parted. Talk about an invitation. And he wasn't about to turn it down—not when he'd waited so long.

He cupped the back of her head with his hand and brought her lips to his. Three years had given him a hunger he hadn't anticipated, and just the touch of her mouth against his brought it roaring to the surface.

There was no thought of delicacy. His tongue thrust into her mouth, finding the silky moisture which did nothing to quench the hunger racing through his body.

Her fingers dug deeply into his shoulders, but he was past feeling pain. Not when he was too busy feasting on the sweetness that was Casey. A part of him sensed she was just as voracious. He pulled her fully onto his lap, pressing her body tightly against his. He wanted her to feel his arousal, for her to know just how famished he was for her. He lifted her shirt so he could feel her bare skin. The heat of her skin had released her perfume until it invaded his nostrils in a heady aroma. Her breasts swelled in his hands as he cupped the satiny orbs.

"Don't stop now," she ordered in a breathy whisper.

"I don't know if I could."

He groaned at the feel of her hands on his bare chest when they burrowed under his shirt. He moaned her name when they trailed with tantalizing slowness over his nipples. But when they started to delve past his waistband, he was positive he was dying and well on his way to heaven.

Jack had to *assume* he was on his way to heaven. He could hear the bells ringing in the distance.

"Jack, are you there?"

The voice may have been soft, but it carried with strong clarity to the patio. Nan. The answering machine had clicked on and now Nan's questions held a censure for them both to hear.

The hammer that struck him wasn't the least bit velvet, but cold, hard steel. The curse he uttered as he leapt to his feet was pithy. The curse Casey screamed when she fell ungracefully to the concrete was equally unladylike.

"Dammit," he muttered, making his way to the house.

Casey slowly got to her feet, rubbing her injured posterior with her hand.

"What are you doing?" she demanded.

He looked over his shoulder. "I'm going to talk to my wife, is what I'm going to do."

Casey shook her head as if she was ridding it of something. "Your *wife?* I was your wife before she was!" she screeched, ignoring his frantic hand waving that asked her to be quiet.

Casey glared at Jack through the patio doorway as he talked on the phone.

"No, Casey and I were just enjoying the evening air on the patio," he said brightly. "How's it going there?"

Casey stared at Jack as if the fury in her eyes could kill him. But then, his death would be too gentle and she wasn't in the mood for gentle deaths. She stood there with her hands on her hips while he finished his phone call and came back outside. The moment he started to open his mouth, she slapped him good and hard across the face.

"There were days I watched some disgusting germs under a microscope. Now I realize they were very tame compared to you," she told him before going off in a huff.

Jack watched her walk away, then he looked over his shoulder at the phone that sat so innocently on the table.

"There is something to be said about bad timing."

"WHO DOES HE THINK he is? The man kisses me senseless, and then he dumps me on the ground like an unwanted package." Casey paced the length of the tiny living room. Her bare feet seemed to stamp holes in the carpet as she walked back and forth in rapid steps. Her face was set in a tight mask that boded ill for anyone who dared come near her. But it was her eyes that betrayed her true feelings. They were laser bright with a fury that seemed to send out sparks with each word she uttered. There would be no doubt in anyone's mind that she was furious and who she was furious with. She slapped her fist against her opposite palm as if it was someone's face she was mentally pounding into the ground. "He deserves to have a root canal without drugs. He deserves an appendectomy without drugs." Her face glowed with malevolence as she imagined the absolute worst. "He deserves to be in a body cast for six months."

"You really want me to suffer, don't you?"

She spun around to face the man standing in her doorway. She silently cursed herself for not locking the door.

"Suffer? Oh, no, I don't want you to suffer." She crossed her arms in front of her chest and curved one leg forward, the toes delicately touching the carpet while the rest of her foot arched upward. "I want you to feel absolute agony." Her smile was bright and as false as plastic. "So, how is Nan? Is she wowing Kansas City with her business expertise?"

"That's not fair, Casey." His eyes were dark and troubled, but at the moment, she didn't seem to care or notice.

"Life's a bitch and so am I," she declared in ringing tones. "This situation isn't fair. Now, if you don't mind, I'd like you to get away from me." She stared at him, her voice and expression cold.

Jack remained standing there just watching her. Then after a few seconds of a standoff, he said quietly, matter-of-factly, "If the phone hadn't rung when it did, I would have had your clothes off and been inside you within seconds. We would have been making love and you would have enjoyed it. No matter how much you deny it, you know it's the truth."

"I'm looking for another place to live" was all she said.

Jack nodded. "Fine, Casey. You've always done what you've wanted. Why should now be any different?"

Chapter Ten

"I'm sorry, Dr. Larson, but we require references, and it appears you are unable to provide them for us," the real estate agent explained. "I understand you've been out of the country for the past few years, but surely you took your credit cards with you?"

And a fat lot of good they would have done her in the jungle, Casey thought. She took a deep breath. The last thing she was going to do was explain the past three years to this woman. "It was a scientific expedition into the Amazon" was all she said.

But Mrs. Anderson's expression was unyielding.

Casey silently reminded herself that there was a name she could give as a reference, and dammit, even though she didn't want to, clearly she had to. She heaved a deep sigh. She'd fallen in love with the small house across the street from the beach she had just walked through. That alone was enough to make her give up the appropriate reference. Quietly she recited Jack's name and address.

"A relative?" Mrs. Anderson asked.

Casey's smile tightened. "My brother."

Within ten minutes after the Realtor had called Jack for verification, Casey had signed all the required paperwork and was presented with the keys.

Afterward, she visited furniture and department stores and soon had everything she needed for her new dwelling. The entire time she was busy choosing towels and sheets, she tried to ignore the pain deep within her body. She knew this was for the best. But if it was, why did it hurt so much?

As she loaded the car with her purchases, she told herself she was doing the right thing. She and Jack needed this kind of distance. Except she didn't want distance. She wanted closeness. She wanted the chance to spend evenings with him. She wanted to find out what books he'd read in the past three years. What he'd done. She blinked rapidly to keep the tears back.

When she returned to the guest house, she noticed Jack's car was parked in the garage. She deliberately didn't look toward the main house as she walked toward the guest cottage. All she needed to do was take one look at him and she'd probably cave in.

"Funny thing," she muttered. "Someone spends three years dreaming of seeing her husband again and then decides to move away." Dropping her purse on the couch, she unbuttoned her blouse and pulled it free from her shorts as she kicked off her sandals. She grabbed a can of Diet Coke from the kitchen, popping the tab and drinking thirstily as she walked

back to the couch and collapsed on it. She rolled her
can against her forehead in hopes of easing the headache that had started pounding in her temples. She
decided self-pity was the cause and aspirin wouldn't
help.

"You didn't waste any time, did you?" Jack commented in a tight voice. He stood in the doorway
looking as if he wasn't sure if she might throw the
can at him.

"What can I say? I walked inside this one little
house and knew it was perfect. It's in a nice, quiet
neighborhood, close to the beach and not too far from
the clinic. I spent the rest of the day shopping for
furniture." She yawned. "I had no idea shopping
could be so tiring."

"I see." He walked in and sat down on the chair
across from her. "I would have thought you'd choose
an apartment instead of a house."

She shook her head. "I want the security of a
house. And this one carries an option to buy. Who
knows, maybe I'll even get a cat."

Jack stared at her as if he didn't recognize the
woman sitting across from him. "You hate cats. You
said they do nothing but shed, aggravate allergies and
disdain all humans."

"I've decided they're not so bad, after all." She
propped her feet up on the coffee table. "They're
pretty self-sufficient, so it might not matter what
hours I might be working." No matter how much she
hurt inside, she was determined to act lighthearted.

She didn't want Jack to know the last thing she wanted to do was leave, even if it was for the best.

"Are you sure it's a good idea for you to work in such a rough area?" he asked.

"After where I've been, it will be like working at Disneyland. At least I won't be a human pincushion for a variety of nasty bugs." Idly, she scratched her arm, then laughed. "See, I talk about it and begin scratching. Want something to drink?"

"I'll get it." He pushed himself out of the chair and walked into the kitchen. He came back with a can of Diet Coke. "I'm sorry, Casey."

She immediately knew what his apology was for.

"It was just one of those things." She shrugged. "The ambience of the evening, too much wine." Not for a million dollars would she admit how much he'd hurt her with his reaction to Nan's phone call. She knew that was why she had gone out and found a place to live. She didn't want to be here when Nan returned and see Jack with her.

She stared straight ahead as she drank her soda. "I can't stay here now, Jack," she said in a low voice. "You know that."

"Yes, I know," he murmured, looking down at his clasped hands.

"I'll act the part of your sister to the best of my ability, but don't ask anything more from me. It wouldn't be fair for either of us." Her voice broke at the end.

"Nan will be back in three days," he said in the same toneless voice.

"By then, I'll be in my house." She leaned forward, setting the soda can on the coffee table. "The furniture will be delivered tomorrow, and after that, all I have to move in is my clothing." She stood up and stretched her arms over her head. "So if you don't mind, I have a lot to do," she said, silently asking him to leave but unable to come right out and say the words.

The silence hanging heavily between them was as charged as the air before a thunderstorm. Casey still hadn't looked at Jack. She couldn't bear to. She could feel his eyes on her, the sensation as strong as if he had physically touched her.

"I hope you'll be willing to part with your phone number when you have your phone installed." There was a sarcastic bite to his words.

"Since I won't know my hours you'll probably have better luck getting hold of me at the clinic."

Jack's motions as he stood up were slow, as if he'd aged many years in the last few moments.

"If that's the way you want it," he said quietly.

"I would say it could be the way Norton might like it," she said, adding a sharp verbal dig. "After all, whatever he asks for, you do. Right? Tell me something, Jack, if Norton demands a grandchild, are you going to oblige him?"

His head swung around and he pierced her with his glare. "Not funny, Casey."

Her smile didn't hold any humor. "Maybe not, but then I'm not the one under his thumb, am I?"

Jack stood up and walked out of the room, slamming the door after him.

"Well, Casey," she said to herself, "you handled that very well." And she promptly burst into tears.

CASEY DIDN'T SEE JACK the following day as she packed her car with most of her clothing. She had already left linens and housewares at the house after her shopping marathon, so she would have less to deal with. She drove over to the house and began carrying clothing and luggage inside. She studied each room with a notepad and pen in her hand, drawing a diagram to help her decide where she wanted the furniture placed. She was determined to do this as orderly as possible. A return to the old Cassandra.

She looked around the small kitchen after she hung curtains in the window over the sink and another set in a small window that overlooked the backyard.

"It's all mine," she murmured, hoisting herself onto the counter as she drank an iced tea she'd picked up at a fast-food restaurant on her way. Old-fashioned glass-front cabinets were now filled with dishware, and appliances lined one counter. "All my doing. No one else's. All mine." She almost burst into tears again. All she could think about was her wish that Jack was here with her.

How badly she had wanted to show him the new Casey. To tell him about her daydreams while in the jungle. What she hoped the two of them would be able to do together. Instead, it was just her.

Casey couldn't remember ever feeling this alone.

JACK PARKED ACROSS the street where he could see Casey's house but he knew she couldn't see him. He pushed the button, watching the window silently glide downward to allow the sea air in. A delivery truck was already backed up to the garage, and two men were carrying a plastic-covered couch through the front door. They reappeared outside, ducked into the back of the truck and came out carrying a coffee table.

"She seems to have everything she needs," he murmured when another truck arrived and two men brought out a television set, stereo system, refrigerator, and washer and dryer and carried them into the house. "Except me." He ignored the note of self-pity in his voice.

Every so often he would catch a glimpse of her standing in the doorway. To his way of thinking, her shorts were too short, and her shirt, knotted just under her breasts, showed too much bare skin. Instead of feathery strands around her face, her hair was slicked back, defining the sharp planes and angles of her face.

What hurt the most was the animation lighting up her face. The excitement of setting up housekeeping. She laughed and chattered away to the deliverymen, who appeared only too happy to accept her attention.

His stomach tightened into a knot of pure acid. Why could she be so nice to everyone else and act as if she wanted to do nothing more than kill him? Dammit, he was her husband! Didn't she remember she was a married woman?

His self-pity was soon overthrown by the righteous anger of a husband watching his wife flirting with strange men.

You forgot something, Jack, a tiny voice inside his head whispered. *How can you feel that way when you don't acknowledge her as your wife in public? She moved away to make it easier for you. But you don't feel so good about it, do you?*

"I hate having a conscience," he muttered, glaring at the small white house with its bright green shutters and door. "She still should know better. Some men might take it the wrong way. They might think she's asking for a late-night visit." His lip curled at the idea of any man even daring to sneak into Casey's bedroom unless it was him.

Wasn't it bad enough she'd cut off all her hair and wore all these clothes that showed more than covered? Wasn't it enough that she wore eye makeup and bright lipstick? Did she have to make him suffer, too?

Jack remained sunk in his depression as he watched the delivery truck depart and a telephone truck pull up in front.

"How did she get service this fast?" he muttered. "I had to wait two weeks." He slumped down in the seat and glared at the truck.

He was so lost in thought that he didn't notice the car pulling up behind him, nor the uniformed man

walking up to the driver's side. He was oblivious until
he heard a knocking against the top of the car. He
looked out at an expressionless face behind mirrored
sunglasses.

"Are you having car trouble, sir?" the police officer asked politely.

"No, officer, I'm just watching my wife move into
her house," he said absently. "No problem at all."

The cop stared at him long and hard. "Your wife?"

Jack nodded, still not thinking anything was wrong.
"She moved in today."

The officer straightened up. "Now, maybe you're
just a nice guy, and then again, maybe you're not.
Either way, you can't park here. So I suggest you
either move along or you go up there and talk to your
wife in a peaceable manner. Maybe you two can work
things out, although—" he looked over his shoulder
"—judging by what's been going in there for the past
couple of hours, I'd say you'll have to do some pretty
good talking. But I don't want to see you still parked
here when I drive by again. Understood?"

Jack's smile dimmed with each word the officer
spoke. He switched on the ignition and put the car in
Drive. "I get the message, Officer."

WHEN CASEY WALKED into the clinic, she felt as if
she had walked into a war zone. The waiting room
was full.

"Gang spat that got out of control," Ron explained
as he approached the reception desk and gathered up

a couple of charts. He handed one to her. "Pick one and use whatever room is free. We don't stand on ceremony here."

Casey called out the name on the top chart, and a young girl stood up, her arm sporting a makeshift bandage.

Casey mustered up the warmest smile she could, considering she wanted nothing more than to gather her up in her arms and assure her nothing bad would happen again. When she finished stitching the arm, she let the girl choose a lollipop out of a large jar Casey had brought in with her.

"Great idea," Greg told her when he walked by. He paused long enough to grab a lollipop and walked on. "You know, of course, the kids will demand to see you from now on." He tore off the wrapper and popped it into his mouth. "Always did like grape." He saluted her with his treat and walked on.

Casey lost track of time as she treated patient after patient. Trina, the R.N., came in when necessary, and Heidi, one of the L.V.N.s, was also there to help her. But by the time the waiting room was empty, it was past two o'clock.

Casey collapsed on one of the examination tables and closed her eyes. They sprang open again when the scent of coffee assaulted her nostrils. She snatched the cup out of Greg's hand and drank greedily. She grimaced at the bitter taste and liquid heat burning her throat.

"Don't tell me, that was my initiation, wasn't it?" she asked.

Greg sat on the stool next to the table. "I honestly didn't expect your first morning to be this hectic."

She shook her head and waved off his apology. "I wanted work and I got it. Since I seem to have a little time, I'm going to empty the car now."

"Need some help?"

"Sure."

Twenty minutes later, the waiting area had magazines, children's books and puzzles, colorful posters and jars of candy. Casey had even purchased a new coffeemaker.

"You don't do anything halfway, do you?" Ron mumbled as he walked in and noted the changes. He shook his head. "You know, from what Greg had said about you—" He stopped, unwilling to go on.

Casey grinned. "He'd better be careful, because I can tell some pretty good stories about him, too."

"I can see we're going to have to talk." He patted her shoulder and walked on.

The balance of the afternoon was quieter than that morning but still busy, so that by evening, Casey felt dead on her feet. As she passed the office, she saw Ron and Greg slouched on the couch with a bottle of whiskey between them.

"Want one?" Greg held up a half-filled glass. "It's purely medicinal."

She shook her head. "I'm for a hot bath instead."

"We stay open later tomorrow night. Would you be willing to come in at noon?" Ron asked.

"For a chance to sleep in, I'll gladly stay late. See you then." She waved a hand over her shoulder as she walked back down the hallway.

By the time she pulled into her garage, Casey considered forgoing the bath and just heading straight for bed. Yawning widely, she staggered into the house and headed for the bedroom, shedding her clothing along the way. By the time she crawled into bed, she was well on her way to dreamland.

"GOOD TO SEE YOU, JACK." Norton greeted his son-in-law with a hearty handshake and slap on the back. "How are you holding up as a bachelor so soon after the wedding?" He guided him through the house and into his den.

When Jack stepped inside the room, he noted the aroma of cigar smoke in the air. Ironic, since he knew Norton was told to stop smoking.

"Makes me appreciate being a married man more," Jack said with a smile. A smile that dimmed when he saw another man seated in a leather chair. A cigar lay burning in an ashtray. "Gerald. What a surprise to see you." He nodded toward the other man.

"Jack." The older man didn't smile.

"What would you like to drink, Jack?" Norton asked, diverting Jack's attention back to him.

"Just club soda, thanks." He took a chair near Gerald.

"How is Nan doing?" Norton asked, pouring the bubbly liquid into an ice-filled glass. He walked over and handed it to Jack. "I still can't believe you allowed her to fly out there without you."

"She's more than qualified to handle those negotiations," Jack said firmly. "I was confident she'd do a much better job than I could. Besides, someone had to stay here."

"You still should have kept her home. If you give her too much latitude in the beginning, she'll think she can do this all the time," the older man warned him in his pompous tone that never failed to raise Jack's hackles.

"You've forgotten one thing, Norton. It's the nineties, and women are showing they have the same abilities we men do," he argued.

"I don't know, Jack." Gerald leaned back in his chair and picked up his cigar, puffing on it. "It seems you have bad luck handling the women in your life. Your first wife dies and now your new wife flies off before the honeymoon is barely over."

Jack stiffened. "That was in very poor taste, Gerald," he said tightly.

Gerald smiled and murmured an apology that didn't sound as sincere as it should have.

"By the way, did your sister tell you about the offer I made her?" he asked abruptly.

"She did." He had an idea where this conversation was going and it wouldn't be pleasant.

Gerald leaned forward, using his cigar to punctuate his words as he spoke. "I must say that Casey has excellent qualifications, and I can see that she would go far with the right backing." There was no doubt he considered himself that backing. "What I don't understand is why she would waste her talent in that poor man's clinic." He shook his head, his expression filled with disgust. "You really should have a good talk with her and explain the facts of life to her."

Now he knew why he was asked here. "I wouldn't worry about that, Gerald. What she didn't learn from her mother was more than covered in medical school."

The older man's expression darkened.

"Think of Casey, Jack," Norton spoke up. His voice cajoled his son-in-law to listen. "Should she really be down there among people who can't appreciate what she can do for them?"

"Of course she shouldn't be!" Gerald boomed. "She doesn't need to waste herself there. Not when you can tell her what good she can do at Oceanview." He sat back, confident that was all that was needed.

Jack's chuckle soon blossomed into full-bodied laughter. The two other men stared at him as if he'd lost his mind.

"I didn't think that was very funny," Gerald said, affronted.

"Oh, Gerald, believe me, it is incredibly hilarious.

Casey has a mind of her own and does what she wants. Besides, if that's what she wants, I'm behind her."

"Then do what's right and stand behind her while she's practicing at Oceanview," Norton urged.

Jack looked from Norton to Gerald, then back to Norton. He hadn't missed the speaking glance that passed between the two men. What were they up to?

"Why is having Casey in your clinic so important to you?" he asked Gerald.

"We have the openings and she's a qualified physician," he replied.

Jack shook his head. "Sorry, that's not good enough." He drained his glass and stood up. "Norton, thank you for the drink. Gerald." He nodded at the other man and walked out.

"We're just trying to help you, Jack," Norton called after him. "We knew you would like to have your sister nearby, and I'm willing to do what's necessary to have that happen."

"And I thank you for it, but I think you've done enough," Jack said as he continued walking out. "Good night."

He sat in his car for several moments, shaking his head as he thought of the men's advice. Norton's words rang a little too harshly in his mind. He feared Casey was right. Norton was controlling him. The older man's arrogance in assuming Jack would make sure Casey moved over to Oceanview was proof of that.

"Can't handle my women? Hell, I can't handle my own life."

CASEY HAD GONE TO BED so tired, she was positive she would sleep like the dead. She hadn't expected to dream—and for all those dreams to be about Jack. When she awoke the next morning, she found her covers tumbled all around her and her body soaked with sweat. She crawled out of bed and made her way to the kitchen, pleased to see her coffeemaker's timer had done what was required and she could instantly pour herself a cup of dark brew. Sipping it, she turned on the shower and adjusted the temperature to hot. Between the coffee and the shower she felt human again.

It was while she fixed herself breakfast that she thought of Jack again. She looked at the phone. Touched it. Hesitated. She took a deep breath and picked it up. Then put it down again when she realized she didn't know his office phone number. She had to dig through her purse for her phone book, then picked up the phone again. Within moments, she was connected with Jack's office.

"Oh, yes, Dr. Larson, your brother asked if you called to put you right through," his secretary told her.

Before Casey could say another word, she heard a click and Jack's voice rolling over the line.

"How are you doing, Casey?" he asked quietly.

"I survived my first day, so I guess you'd have to

say I'm fine," she said just as quietly. "How about you?" Was this what they were left with, she asked herself, clichéd conversation?

"I'm doing fine. By the way, I saw Gerald last night. He couldn't believe you turned down his offer in order to work in a walk-in clinic." He chuckled. "He seemed pretty insulted. He acted as if you might have lost your mind."

She shrugged, then realized he couldn't see her action. "With the size of his ego, he would think that. How did you happen to run into him?"

"Norton asked me over for a drink last night."

"Ooh, an evening with the father-in-law," she cooed. "That must have been interesting."

"What was interesting was Gerald being there," Jack said.

Casey halted the motion of lifting her coffee cup to her lips. "His being there was obviously deliberate. Good old Gerald must not be used to rejection. Doesn't he understand rejection can be good for the soul? He just might learn how to be a better person because of it."

"More like according to him, you'd be the better person for taking the position. He wants me to talk you into reconsidering."

She dropped two slices of bread into the toaster. "He does, does he? What did you tell him?"

"What do you think I told him? I told him you have a mind of your own and you do what you want.

I guess I should have told him that the last person you'd listen to would be me,'' he said ruefully.

"It wouldn't matter. So tell me, is Norton still looking spry?'' She couldn't resist asking.

She could hear his hesitation. "He looked fine.''

"Amazing how a man who was on his deathbed not so long ago is doing so well now,'' she commented. "I'm sorry, Jack, but I need to get to the clinic. If you get a chance one day, why don't you stop by and see exactly what we do. Then you can report back to the Big Brothers.''

"Not funny, Casey.''

"Did I say I was trying to be funny?'' she asked innocently. "I'm not the one with all these guardians. Speaking of guards, have you heard from Nan lately?''

She could hear his muttered curse. "Do you have anything else to say?''

"No.''

"I have a meeting.''

"Remember, Jack, don't let them take you over,'' she warned. "Pod people tend to do that and before you know it, you've lost your soul.''

"Goodbye, Casey.''

She hung up and stared at the phone. "I just hope you can save yourself before it's too late.''

JACK DIDN'T HAVE a meeting. After he disconnected the call, he leaned back in his chair and thought about what had been going on. He still puzzled over Norton and Gerald's insistence that Casey work at the center. Why was it all coming down to him?

He felt another load on his shoulders as he thought of all that had happened since Casey reappeared. And even before that.

Norton's heart attack. All the older man had done for him before then. What Jack owed him and, in a sense, what Jack owed Nan. She'd resolutely pulled him back to life by taking him to social events and browbeating him into actually enjoying himself. He felt as if it was all up to him now. And if it was up to him, what about Casey? The more he thought about her, the more he realized just how important she was to him.

Even now, with both of them having changed so much, he still felt that connection between them. A connection so strong it could only mean one thing.

"So, idiot, if you love Casey so much, why are you married to Nan?"

Chapter Eleven

Casey couldn't help herself. While her work kept her more than busy, a part of her still looked around for a familiar dark-haired man. She thought for sure Jack would stop by the clinic. But as the days passed and there was still no sign of him, she'd begun to give up hope. The regret she felt wasn't surprising. She was coming to realize she wasn't as angry at him as she liked to say she was.

"What about Jonathon?" Greg's question brought an end to her daydreaming.

She looked up at him, confusion in her eyes. He stood in front of her in the office, a steaming mug of coffee in his outstretched hand to help her relax after the long day. "Excuse me?"

"I said, I'm surprised Jonathon doesn't mind you working here. I mean, weird hours, not exactly well-heeled patients." He slanted her a glance. "Especially when his wife is so wealthy."

Casey's mug froze just before touching her lips.

Greg smiled at her stunned expression. "Give me

a break, Casey. I do read the newspaper now and then. Even I couldn't miss the pretty big spread on Jonathon's marriage to a wealthy socialite.'' He deliberately stared at the plain gold band she wore on her left hand's third finger.

Casey could feel the flush creeping up her face, burning it a dark red. ''Does anyone else know?''

He shook his head. ''No one has ever said anything, so I don't think so. But then, all you've ever said is that you're married, not any specifics.''

''It's a very strange story,'' she muttered. ''He thought I was dead and he married Nan.''

''But he's still married to her?'' He twisted around to face her. ''Casey, I may be a doctor and not a lawyer, but even I know the word for that kind of situation is *bigamy*.''

Casey drank her coffee in a deliberate attempt to delay her explanation. How much should she say? And would her explanation sound as crazy to him as it honestly did to her?

''It's complicated,'' she began.

Greg merely raised an eyebrow, silently indicating for her to continue. Casey took a deep breath.

''Is anyone in here?''

She considered the slurred voice a blessed interruption to a conversation she didn't wish to pursue. She rejoiced in the intervention, even if the voice sounded a little too familiar and not one she cared to hear at that moment. She pasted a false smile on her lips as she set her mug down on the floor and hopped off the couch.

"Now what?" Greg muttered, getting to his feet. "Just what we need. A drunk to make the evening complete."

Casey held up her hand to halt him. "Don't worry, I'll take care of it." She hurried down the hallway.

"No way am I going to let you go out there by yourself. They can get nasty at times." He was fast on her heels.

Casey almost lost her balance when Greg crashed into her back as she skidded to a stop before the intruder.

Greg looked over her shoulder and gasped. "Jonathon?"

"Jack, what are you doing here?" Casey asked, sounding calmer than she felt. She reached behind her and used her elbow to push Greg back as hard as she could. She ignored his grunt of pain as her elbow connected to his stomach.

A disheveled Jack swayed from side to side in front of her. His tie hung askew from his shirt collar, and his shirt was unbuttoned halfway down his chest. He stared at her bleary-eyed.

"You tol' me to come by so I could see you working," he stated in the slow, measured tones of a man who is trying to convey he hasn't had too much to drink. "That's why I'm here."

"You're drunk," she said flatly, although it was obvious it didn't take a doctor to make that diagnosis.

Jack swayed from one way to the other, almost losing his balance and just barely catching himself in time. "Am not. I'm just very relaxed." He squinted at the figure standing behind her. He waved at the man standing behind Casey. "Hey, is that Greg? Hi, Greg. How the hell are you?"

Casey heaved a deep sigh. "I'm going to kill him."

"I wouldn't worry," Greg said, amusement lacing his voice. "He's going to wish he was dead when he wakes up tomorrow. Hi, there, Jonathon. You look different."

"That's cuz I don't use that name anymore. Everybody calls me Jack." He shook his head exaggeratedly. His smile was comical. "Casey tol' me to come by and see what she does. I even brought her something." He held up a large bag of butter-toffee peanuts. "You always liked them."

For one brief second, her heart melted at his remembering what she had said that evening, how much she'd craved the peanuts when she was in the jungle. Just as quickly, it hardened again. How dare he show up in this condition!

"I don't think this was a good time for you to come by, Jack." She looked around and glared at Greg. "Do you mind?"

"Not at all." His face twisted as he tried to suppress his chuckle. "I never thought I'd see the uptight Jonathon falling-down drunk. This is fascinating."

Casey swung back to Jack. "You didn't drive here in this condition, did you?" she demanded.

He shook his head again. "Couldn't find my keys, so I called a taxi. The driver said it wasn't a good idea to come here late at night, but you weren't home, so I knew you were here. I tol' him you were a doctor, so we were safe." He smiled as if expecting praise for his brilliant deduction. "Where's all the patients?"

Casey muttered a pithy curse. "I don't believe this." She looked toward Greg, whose mouth was still twitching with mirth. "Help me get him into my car." She grabbed Jack by one of his arms.

"See, I knew you'd wanna see me." He smacked his lips at her, expelling a potent breath of whiskey. "Give us a kiss."

Casey screwed up her face and turned away. "Not in this lifetime. Dammit, Greg, take his other arm!" she snapped at him.

"Yes, Doctor," he said with a solemnity that had her itching to deck him.

Jack looked around. "Where we goin'?" he muttered as they dragged him back outside.

"I'm taking you home, Jack," she said between gritted teeth, practically pushing him against the passenger side of the car. When he started to slide toward the ground, she grabbed his arm again. "Greg, keep him upright while I unlock the door."

"So Jack, why were you drinking tonight?" Greg asked in a conversational tone.

Jack looked at him in a bleary-eyed stare. "I thought you were a real piece of scum for taking my wife away from me. But if you hadn't taken her away from me, we wouldn't have been out here like this.'' He held out his arms. ''Casey came back to me, but look, she's back with you, too.'' He shook his head in wonderment. ''Damn, we just seem to go round and round, don't we?''

Greg's laughter was abruptly stifled when he found Casey glaring at him. ''Believe me, next time you can spend three years in a jungle with her,'' he told Jack.

Jack shook his head as he tried to assimilate what Greg said. He stared at him bug-eyed. ''You were in a jungle with my wife? When?''

''Oh, for God's sake,'' Casey muttered, prodding him none too gently into the passenger seat. When Jack fumbled with the seat belt, she reached across him and made sure it was tight as possible. She straightened up and turned around. ''Not one word,'' she warned, holding up her forefinger to forestall anything Greg was ready to say.

Before he could say anything, she walked around to the driver's door and opened it. She winced as an off-key version of ''Achy Breaky Heart'' assaulted the air. ''Shut up, Jack,'' she ordered, climbing in.

Greg stood there, watching Casey as she peeled out of the parking lot.

''I'd sure hate to be Jack when he sobers up because she's going to kill him.''

''JACK, I SWEAR IF YOU don't shut up I will stuff your shirt down your throat,'' Casey threatened as she pulled him out of the car. How many broken-heart songs could she endure? "You have to help me here." She jabbed him in the side as she pushed and prodded him through the garage and through the back door.

"Wow, there's a lot of color in here," Jack said, looking around the kitchen after Casey flipped on the light. He swayed back and forth on his feet.

"Sit there," she ordered, pushing him into one of the chairs at the table.

Jack squinted at Casey as she opened the refrigerator and withdrew a jug of orange juice. She filled a glass and thrust it at him. "Drink this down." She pulled out a bottle from a cabinet and shook out two tablets. She held them out in her palm.

"What're they?" he asked, eyeing them suspiciously.

"Aspirin. Take them. They'll help you feel better in the morning." She pushed them at him again. "Though, I don't know why I care."

Jack complied. "You know, I'm really tired."

"You can sleep on the couch."

"But I wanted to watch you work," he mumbled as they made their way into the living room, where Jack fell back onto the couch.

"Take off your shoes," she told him as she went into the bedroom and came out with a pillow and blanket. She set them on the end of the couch and studied him. She never thought she'd see Jack so disheveled and just plain out of control. This wasn't the man she knew so well.

His movements were clumsy as he pushed off his loafers and pulled his tie off. He dropped all three to the floor.

"I only went there because you told me to," he muttered.

Casey tried to close her eyes to what she knew she should do, but the effort was useless. She rummaged through her black bag until she pulled out a small glass vial and a disposable syringe.

"Drop your pants, Jack."

He grinned sloppily. "I knew you still liked me."

She inserted the needle into the vial and withdrew some of the liquid. "Don't get any ideas, buster," she warned. "I'm just doing the nice thing before I change my mind." She pushed the syringe up a bit until she knew there were no air bubbles in the hypodermic.

Jack stood up and unbuckled his belt. He pushed down his slacks and briefs, then turned around.

Casey stared at his rear end, mesmerized by the tight, hard flesh before her. She hated herself for enjoying the view.

"This won't hurt, will it? Ow!" he screamed.

Casey smiled, swabbing the affected area with an alcohol-soaked piece of cotton. "Oops, I guess I should have been more careful where I aimed the needle," she apologized without a bit of sympathy. "But the vitamin B shot will help your hangover."

"I never get hangovers," he denied, dropping back on the couch. He yelped when his injured posterior made contact with the couch. He shot her a pained look and adjusted his position. He pushed the pillow under his head and covered himself with the blanket. Within moments he was sound asleep.

"You never get drunk, so you have no idea how you'll feel in the morning," she told him, pausing long enough to adjust his covering.

She headed to the bathroom with the intention of relaxing in a tub of hot water. She had just settled herself in the cinnamon-scented bubbles when she realized her usual sense of peace and quiet was missing.

"I don't believe this!" she groaned.

The gravelly sound of Jack's snores easily penetrated the closed door and seemed to bounce off the walls.

Casey had to ask herself why she was bothering to put up with this charade. When she and Jack should be planning a new life together, he was with another woman.

She knew it was because he'd always been too much of a Boy Scout. Someone played on his sense of loyalty and he just went along with whatever they said. Jack needed her to keep him in line. "Dammit, he just needs me," she cried, blinking furiously to stem the tears threatening to fall. "And I need him because I love him." She glared at the door that hid the sight of her peacefully sleeping husband. "The idiot."

When Casey finally went to bed, she lay awake listening to Jack's snoring. She found the sound comforting, but she would never admit it to him.

Half asleep, she thought she heard the shower running, but she could have dreamed it for all she knew. She snuggled farther under the covers and dug her face deeper into her pillow.

She mumbled an incoherent sentence when she felt the bed shift and the cool air as the covers were lifted then dropped back down. Almost instantly, she felt bare skin against her back.

"Hey there."

Still in that hazy world of sleep, Casey automatically curled her arms around a pair of hard shoulders that felt damp to her skin.

"You smell good, woman," a male voice murmured in her ear.

She drifted down further until she entered a dream room filled with the largest bed she had ever seen. She just happened to be lying in the middle of that bed—and Jack was bending over her. Both of them were naked. She decided she liked black satin sheets. Especially with Jack lying on them and doing all those delicious things to her.

"Mmm," she murmured throatily. She wanted to enjoy her dream Jack as she felt a pair of lips travel along her nape and across the top of her back. She sleepily giggled and shifted her shoulders under the marauding lips. Then she started to purr when she felt a slightly rough palm cup her breast and a thumb circle her nipple. The dream was getting pretty hot. Hot and incredible. If she wasn't sleeping she would have thought Jack was in bed with her.

"You feel so good," her dream Jack whispered in her ear just before he began nibbling on her earlobe.

Casey smiled in her sleep as she turned over to allow her dream Jack more access. His murmured words of praise for her body was like a heady drug. Lips pressed against her belly elicited another sigh. Hands caressing her inner thighs prompted her to part them. She moaned as he probed her entrance. She rotated her hips, lifting them as pleasure traveled upward.

"Let me love you, Casey," her phantom Jack murmured.

She could say yes. It didn't matter since she was in the midst of a dream that was hotter than any of her dreams in the jungle.

It might have been more than three years since she had made love, but the sensation was still there. Even stronger, more electric. She gasped at the fullness stretching her, the heat of a man's body searing her skin. She grabbed his shoulders and lifted her hips at the same time he thrust inside her again.

A part of Casey's mind marveled that the fire could be felt so strongly in a dream. She noted the minty heat of his breath, the rough satin of his skin against hers and earthy words filling her mind.

When fire burst through her body, she felt catapulted into space. At the same time, her brain finally realized that this wasn't a dream. There was actually a man in her bed making love to her! Her eyes snapped open and she stared into Jack's eyes. His face was tight with desire as he looked down on her.

Casey didn't know what to say or do. At the moment, it didn't matter. Her body had already taken over. She grasped Jack's shoulders and wrapped her legs around his thighs as she felt herself thrust high into the heavens. She felt his body tighten and then his heady release.

"I think I just found the perfect cure for a hangover," he muttered.

She collapsed against her pillow, feeling as if she had just gotten off a roller coaster. She willed her breathing to slow and her mind to figure out what just happened.

"I thought I was dreaming," she whispered, still feeling her heart hammer against her chest.

"You sure didn't act like you were dreaming," Jack teased gently.

Casey turned her head. "I feel as if I just finished the ultimate roller-coaster ride." She could feel her smile stretching her lips. She didn't think she could ever stop smiling.

"Honey, you just told a man what he wants to hear." He began nibbling on her ear.

She closed her eyes and tipped her head closer to his marauding lips. "This is so much better than any dream," she moaned as his teeth closed tenderly on her earlobe at the same time his palm covered her belly. His hand rubbed delicate circles on the taut skin, which caused her breath to catch.

"This time you're going to know this isn't any dream," he told her just before his mouth covered hers.

Casey was again lost in that sensual whirlwind as Jack entered her with a thrust so deep that it brought a moan to her lips and a groan of satisfaction to his. She hooked her legs around his upper thighs and moved with him in a rhythm old as time. What they'd shared years before was pallid compared to the firestorm they generated now. Their mouths locked as their damp bodies strained for that last summit. When they reached it, their movements quickened until they both felt as if they had been transported to another galaxy. This time, when Jack lay back, he rolled Casey into his arms. She automatically looped a leg over his upper thigh and rested her cheek against his chest. She idly combed the damp hair blanketing his chest. She couldn't stop herself from smiling. And why not? Now she knew that he had finally made his choice and she was that choice! She wasn't going to be alone in the house after all.

"This can't get any better," she murmured, using her nails to scratch the damp skin and slowly trail downward until she reached her destination.

He hissed a curse. "Dammit, Casey. Are you trying to kill me?"

"Kill you?" She arched an eyebrow. The smile on her lips was that of an extremely satisfied woman who was aware of her power. "But if I did that, how could I ravish you?" She braced herself on one arm so she could lean over him. "And that, my dear, is exactly what I intend to do to you all day." She drew out the last two words, which held a great deal of sensual promise. She glanced at the bedside clock. "There's no reason to even get out of bed. It's only ten." Her lips traced the curve of his upper lip.

"Ten!" Jack shot up in bed so swiftly, Casey fell back. "Dammit! Nan's flight is due in at noon." He leapt out of bed and bent down to grab his clothing that was scattered on the floor.

Casey couldn't admire the delectable sight of a very firm male backside when she was feeling the disgruntled emotion of one who has been rejected—again. She had forgotten that Jack had another life. An oversight she hated herself for submitting to. A situation that shouldn't have happened in the first place.

"I told her I'd pick her up," Jack said, pulling on his briefs, then his slacks. He threw on his shirt and tucked it unbuttoned into his slacks.

Casey sat up, pulling the sheet up to her neck. She suddenly felt as if her nakedness was obscene. She wasn't sure whether to cry or get angry. She opted for the latter.

"Don't come back to the clinic again, Jack," she said in a voice devoid of emotion. "Or here."

Jack must have heard the finality in her voice because he looked up. He understood immediately what he had done to her. He had the grace to look sheepish.

"Casey—"

She shook her head, refusing to hear him. "Don't say anything now because it won't do any good," she told him. "Just get out and leave me alone." She lay back down with her back to him.

She could just barely see him in the mirror on her dresser and noticed he started to lean over as if to say something, but he stopped himself before he gave in to his impulse. Instead, he turned away and walked quietly out the door.

A moment later, she could hear him on the phone in the kitchen asking for a taxi to pick him up. She remained curled up in bed as she listened to his footsteps in the kitchen. A part of her hoped he would come back into the bedroom in an attempt to clear the air, but he never did.

Ten minutes later she heard a car horn honk from outside, then the sound of her front door opening and closing.

Casey had no idea how long she lay huddled under the covers after he left. All she knew was that she hurt. Her entire body hurt. The pleasurable aches from their lovemaking seemed to mock her. The agony tearing her heart apart was what she concentrated on to keep from thinking of the past couple of hours. That same agony helped her climb out of bed and go into the bathroom, where she stood under a hot shower, scrubbing herself until all traces of Jack were gone from her skin. If tears streamed down her cheeks she wouldn't know, because the shower spray whisked away what she had treasured.

Chapter Twelve

No one could have hated Jack more than he hated himself that morning. He called himself every name in the book, but it didn't help ease the pain deep inside him.

He returned home and took a quick shower, even though the last thing he wanted to do was wash Casey's scent from his skin. He stood under the water spray with his head bowed under the spray and his hands braced against the tile.

"I hate what my life has come to."

He pulled clothing from the closet and drawers and tossed them on the bed as he dressed.

"Tell Nan the truth about Casey," he ordered himself, picking up his socks.

"Dammit, I always lived a normal boring life," he muttered to himself as he jerked on a deep-teal-colored polo shirt and tucked it into tan twill slacks. "Never had a book overdue at the library. Was polite to my elders. I was so typical I was downright boring. Now look what I've done." He practically crammed his wallet into his slacks back pocket and snatched up his keys. "You need to do something about this right now, Larson," he told himself as he hurried down the stairs. "It can't go on any longer."

As he drove to the airport, he mulled over how to tell Nan the truth about Casey. Even though he had showered, he felt as if her scent still clung to his skin. His fingertips itched with the memory of her skin quivering under his touch. Her mouth trembling under his, tasting sweet as sin. Her body wrapped around his as she— A car horn and a shouted curse brought him back to the present. He turned the wheel sharply to bring his car back into the proper lane.

"That's all I'd need," he muttered, flipping on his turn signal. "Two wives at my funeral. Of course, it would mean I wouldn't have to tell Nan. And Casey would be furious she wouldn't have a chance to kill me, after all."

Jack pulled into the airport lot and parked the car. He stepped out and inhaled the strong scent of jet and automobile exhaust. With his sunglasses settled on his nose, the view was a faint gray tone as he looked around. He walked across the expansive parking lot toward the terminal. A glance at his watch told him he was close to a half hour early, but that was fine with him. He'd use that time to think about what he planned to say to Nan. Still, one part of his brain whispered, did he want to just blurt it out? After all, she'll be tired from her trip. She'll be terribly vulnerable. Would it be right to just hit her across the eyes with the news the moment she got off her flight?

"You're a wimp, Larson," he muttered, walking into the terminal. "No wonder Casey threw you out. You don't deserve her."

As it was, Jack didn't have time to prepare himself. According to the arrivals board, Nan's flight was early and would be landing in five minutes. Jack double-checked the gate number and hurried down the con-course. By the time he arrived, the jet was taxiing up to the gate. Jack stood near the door watching the passengers disembark.

Nan, looking cool and beautiful, was one of the last people to come through the door, with Dan right be-hind her. Her head was partially turned as she said something to him. When she turned back around and spied Jack, her eyes mirrored surprise. Her lips stretched in a broad smile.

"Darling, how sweet of you to pick me up," she greeted him with a hug and kiss.

"Last I recall, you'd asked me to," he said dryly. His nose tickled at the muskier perfume radiating from her skin. "New perfume?"

"Something I found in Chicago," she replied. "We finished early so I took a few days in Chicago for some shopping."

"The woman may not shop often, but when she does..." Dan shook his head and groaned.

"How did you do out there?" Jack asked the other

man. "Did you get any nibbles on your Midwest job hunt?"

He shrugged. "Some interviews. You never know."

"Don't listen to him. He was very helpful at the office with me," Nan said as they walked toward the baggage claim area. "I told Dan he should have put an application in with us, but he said he didn't want to be hired because of nepotism."

"Can't have them thinking I got the job because I'm related to the boss," Dan said lightly, walking on Nan's other side.

"Nonsense," she scoffed. She looked up at Jack. "I told him to put an application in with Human Resources first thing Monday. He doesn't have to say he's related to me. I'm sure they'll hire him."

"I didn't know we had any openings for a computer programmer," Jack commented.

"If we don't, I'm sure they'll find something for him," she said confidently.

They stopped by the baggage carousel.

"Why don't I bring the car around while you two get the luggage," Jack suggested.

"Great," Dan approved. "Don't worry, I'll help Nan with the heavy stuff."

Jack couldn't resist it. He flashed Dan a smile worthy of a shark on the prowl. "You do that."

As he walked out, he mulled over the conversation. He had a feeling that while Dan glibly said he didn't want to be hired just because he's related to the head of the company, it didn't mean he wouldn't play on that connection if it made things easier for him.

"Maybe I should fix him up with Casey," he said out loud as he neared his car. "She'd whip him into shape in no time. Either that or kill him." That prospect cheered him immensely by the time he parked the car outside of the crowded baggage claim area.

"The first thing I want when we get home is a nice, long hot bath." Nan sighed with relief when she settled herself in the passenger seat. "And something cold to drink. Flying seems to suck all the fluid out of my skin." She half turned to Jack. "Were there any problems here?"

"Not a one," he cheerfully lied, only because it seemed the thing to do.

"How's your lovely sister doing?" Dan asked from the back seat.

"Why didn't she come with you?" Nan asked.

"She's probably working today." He'd already decided this wasn't the time to set the record straight.

"Working? Gerald said he was going to offer her a position at Oceanview," she said, delighted.

"He offered, but she didn't accept."

Nan frowned. "What?"

Jack waited until he raced onto the freeway before answering. "She didn't take his job. She's working in a free clinic farther down the coast."

"A free clinic?" She said the words as if they tasted bad. "Why would she want to do that?"

"A former colleague helps run it, and she went down to see it and decided to stay. She also found a house to rent and moved out about a week ago." Those were words he hated saying because he hated to admit she wasn't close by.

"So little sister decided she wanted to be out on her own," Dan mused. "I can understand that. She probably would feel odd if she entertained her dates while her big brother is just across the yard."

"She's working too hard to have dates," Jack growled.

"There's no woman who works too hard she doesn't have time to party. It just takes the right man to convince her."

Nan turned to frown at her cousin. "Dan, don't tease."

Jack's mind conjured up a much stronger warning.

"I don't see why Casey would give up the opportunity to align herself with Gerald's medical group," Nan went on. "What can this clinic offer her?"

"A challenge," Jack murmured. Somehow he didn't remember very much of his previous night's visit to the clinic. But his actions that morning rang loud and clear in his memory. Colors, textures, tastes were still vivid, but he wished they weren't. They made him feel even worse about the situation he was in.

"Have you spoken to Daddy lately?" Nan asked, unwittingly interrupting his thoughts. "I tried to call him last night but he wasn't in."

"No, I haven't talked to him the past few days," he replied, remembering the last time he'd seen his father-in-law and the reason behind that visit. One that still puzzled him.

"I hope he's all right," she mused. "Did he seem well when you saw him?"

"Well enough to slug back a shot of whiskey," he told her.

"He shouldn't be drinking!" she said, shocked. "I had hoped he would take care of himself while I was gone. I'll call him as soon as we get home."

Jack thought of the pair of ears in the back seat and thought about not saying anything just then. He'd wait until he and Nan were alone.

"Well, Dan, since Casey has moved out of the guest house, I guess there's no reason why you can't move in there," he told the other man. "Unless, of course, you'd rather find a place of your own."

"I'm not proud. I'll take it," Dan said happily.

Jack's hands tightened their grip on the steering wheel. He just knew Dan would look perfect with a broken jaw.

"NAN, WE NEED TO TALK about something before you call your father," Jack said when they deposited her bags in her bedroom.

She stopped and looked at him inquiringly. "Is there something you haven't told me, Jack? Is Daddy back in the hospital and you didn't want to tell me before?"

He shook his head. "No, he's fine. It's about the last time I saw him. Gerald was over there, too. They were pressuring me to convince Casey to give up her work at the walk-in clinic."

Nan looked confused. "I don't see what's so wrong with that. From what you've said I can't imagine that clinic is a good atmosphere for her."

Jack felt every muscle in his body tighten. "Nan, Casey has a mind of her own and I respect her for that." He hadn't realized the words came out harsh until he saw the surprise flare in Nan's eyes. She straightened up to the perfect posture she was known for.

"There's no need to browbeat me, Jack," she said quietly. "I'm sure Daddy was only thinking of Casey's welfare."

"I apologize if you thought I was browbeating you, Nan," he said. "Believe me, Casey can look after herself."

"Perhaps if I talk to her," she offered.

He suddenly felt tired. "She might not appreciate it."

"Oh, darling, you just don't understand women, do you," she teased lightly. "Casey might take it better coming from a woman. I'm going to call Daddy." She pressed her lips against his cheek. "And don't worry, I forgive you." She opened her bedroom door, went inside and closed it behind her.

Jack stood there, feeling as if he'd been outwitted, somehow.

"I should have told her."

"HOW WAS YOUR DAY OFF, princess?" Greg asked Casey when she walked into their shared office. He flinched when she dropped her backpack on the floor and kicked it under her desk. "Oops, sorry I asked."

She turned around. "Would the word *neuter* give you a hint?"

His face lost all color at her statement. "The hangover wasn't punishment enough?"

"Barely. Now, if you don't mind, I'm going to make some coffee and get out there. I see the waiting room is packed."

Casey stopped by her office first and dropped down into her chair. She braced her elbows on her desk and covered her face with her hands.

She didn't want to think about Jack. She had done enough of that yesterday while crying in the shower. That hadn't stopped her from crying while she pulled the sheets off the bed and threw them in the washer. Even after the sheets were washed and dried, she realized she couldn't sleep on them again without thinking about Jack, so she dropped them off at a Goodwill drop box.

A part of her had hoped all day he would call her. She tried to tell herself it was only so she could salvage her pride by hanging up on him, but she knew that wasn't the truth.

Casey remembered the easy lovemaking early in their marriage and the lovemaking that would naturally happen as their marriage progressed. But she had never experienced anything like the explosive lovemaking between them the day before. Was it because of a three-year abstinence? Or was it the result of her dreams in the jungle?

She groaned as she felt her breasts tighten at the memory of his touch and the hot moisture of his mouth on her skin. At the moment, she wanted nothing more than a long, cold shower—and even then she doubted it would help.

"Men should be locked in a closet where they stay until we need them and then we can lock them back up after we're finished with them," she muttered.

"Would we have cable TV in there? It would make it a lot easier."

Casey looked up to find Greg standing there, clearly pleased he'd caught her unaware.

"We gotta have all the sports channels," he said, stepping inside. "I'm never happy unless I have my ESPN."

"You are a very sick man," she stated.

"Gee, thanks for the diagnosis, Doctor." He grabbed a chair, turned it around and sat straddling it.

"Okay, tell Papa."

"Tell Papa?" she repeated. "I don't think so."

"You'll feel better," he urged.

Casey stood up and walked over to Greg. She smiled and patted him on the cheek.

"Talking to you would only make it worse," she informed him before she walked out of the office.

Casey was grateful her morning was busy as she

went from diagnosing mumps to treating colds and setting a broken arm.

Greg touched her arm as they passed by in the hall. "How about sneaking out of here for lunch? My treat."

She shrugged. "All right, but only if you don't try your 'tell papa' routine again."

"I'm even going to take you to a café that's your style," he told her as they walked outside to his truck.

Casey shook her head. "Greg, your idea of gourmet food is fajitas."

"Sweetheart, you'll be eating those words very soon."

Ten minutes later, Casey was looking around the patio of a beautiful beachfront café.

"I gather you and Jack didn't kiss and make up after he woke up the next day?" Greg ventured.

Casey swallowed a gulp of iced tea so fast she almost choked. Greg helpfully slapped her on the back. Still choking, she waved him off.

"I guess that means you did kiss and make up," he said, returning to his chair. He offered her a look of sympathy. "I'm sorry, Casey."

"Why? Because he's stupid enough to give in to his new wife," she said bitterly. "I can't believe he wants to stay with her. Just as I can't believe Norton has one foot in the grave. If that man has a serious heart condition, I should go back to medical school. Nothing seems to fit."

"Wait a minute," Greg held up his hand. "What exactly does Norton Xavier have to do with this?"

"Not just him, but Gerald Montgomery," she explained as she nibbled on her omelette. "You'd think Oceanview Medical Center would fold if I didn't join them. They even put the pressure on Jack to talk me into taking it."

"What does the head of an electronics firm and the head of a medical center have to do with you?" he asked.

"I'm Norton's son-in-law's baby sister." She struck a model's pose. "Which I guess I'll always be." She looked as if she wanted to throw her fork across the table, then she carefully set it down on her plate.

Greg shook his head. "I don't know, Casey, but this isn't you. You're basically letting them walk all over you. One person stole your husband and you're letting her keep him. Two others want you to take a job you don't want and they're even pressuring Jack to pressure you more. What happened to that fighter I defended myself against down in the Amazon? You're really not going to let them win, are you?"

Casey stared at Greg, stunned by his attack.

"Are you?" he pressed. "Come on, Casey. You can't tell me you're going to take this whimpering? What about that rusty scalpel you're always talking about?"

She sat up straighter. "He was mine first."

Greg nodded eagerly.

"And she's totally wrong for him."

He nodded again.

"Not to mention she's got a secret of her own that I doubt she'd want her dear daddy to find out about," she went on. Energized, she started eating again. She was clearly gathering her strength. "You're right, Greg."

"Yes!" Greg pumped his fist up and down in the air.

Casey's eyes shone with ferocious fervor. "When they get through with me, they won't know what hit them."

Chapter Thirteen

Nan was positive something was wrong with Jack. She couldn't put her finger on it, but she could sense a difference in him since she'd returned. She finally aired her thoughts out loud one afternoon.

"So he's acting out of sorts," Dan said lazily, lounging in one of the chairs on the patio. "Maybe it's the lack of sex. Not that you're lacking for any, even if it's not coming from the groom." He shot her a smug smile.

"Stop acting like a jerk, Dan," she snapped. "If Jack had one little hint you weren't my cousin, this entire marriage would blow up in my face and Daddy would make sure I never took over the company."

"So why are you ticked off that your hubby doesn't want to hit the sheets with you?" Dan asked, sounding irked.

"What if Daddy finds out things aren't right between us? He'll think there's something wrong and he'll automatically think it's me," she told him with an edge in her voice as she paced back and forth.

Dan tipped his sunglasses down his nose to watch her for a moment, then used his forefinger to push them back up. "I thought Daddy Dearest had a bad heart."

She immediately rounded on him. "Don't you wish anything bad on him!"

He reared back from her attack. "But then you'd have the company all to yourself and you can divorce Jack and marry me."

She ran her fingers through her hair, destroying the careful coiffure from that morning. "Dan, I couldn't divorce Jack right away no matter what. It wouldn't look right. We'd have to wait for a suitable length of time."

He snorted. "One excuse after another. That's all I hear anymore. I don't appreciate hanging around as your cousin, Nan. What if Norton finally realizes I'm not a relation?"

"I told you. He's always hated my mother's family, so you're perfectly safe as long as you don't say something wrong. Which you are known to do," she reminded him, wagging her finger in his face.

"So I had a few too many drinks," he tried to excuse himself. "No one noticed."

"But someone could have." Her lovely face was tight with anger. "And I also want you to stop making remarks about Casey."

"What's wrong with that? She's pretty and single. Like me," he said pointedly.

Nan didn't have to say anything to him. The expression on her face said it all.

"Just don't make any more mistakes," she warned him before walking into the house.

"You know, Nan, you can be a real bitch sometimes," he shouted after her.

"In this household, that term can only be attributed to a female dog." A male voice sounded from behind.

Dan half turned in his chair. His face paled when he saw the man.

"Hey there, cousin-in-law," he greeted Jack with a broad grin. "Don't sweat it. It's nothing more than a family spat."

Jack walked over to Dan and leaned over the chair, placing a hand on each chair arm, effectively trapping the man.

"I don't give a damn about family spats," he said in a quiet voice that was more menacing than a shout. "No woman deserves being called that name. I suggest first you go inside and apologize to Nan, then you pack up and get out tonight." He straightened up.

"You can't throw me out," Dan said with a show of bravado.

"Yes, I can."

Jack walked into the house and found Nan in the family room busily plumping up the pillows on the couch. She was muttering something under her breath he couldn't quite make out. He had an idea it had to do with Dan.

"Are you all right?" he asked.

She looked up, surprised by his question. "Of course, why wouldn't I be?"

Jack was used to a fragile Nan except when she was in the office, so what he saw now appeared to be a new side to her.

"Nothing. I'm going up to take a shower." He turned to leave. He figured while he was showering he could try to figure out what prompted Dan to snap at Nan and why Dan appeared so worried that he might have overheard more of the conversation.

"Dinner will be ready in an hour," she called after him. "I have it in the oven now."

"Fine."

Jack went upstairs and went into his bedroom. The first thing he did was look outside. He noticed Dan hadn't moved from his chair.

He had to admit he hadn't liked the man from the beginning. He saw him as a leech. Someone who would look for the main chance. He even doubted Dan had been looking for work. Why should he when he had his cousin paying his bills? Jack would be glad to see the last of him.

He stood under the shower, enjoying the hot stream of water flowing down on him. He was finding he could do his best thinking while in the shower. Of course, lately his thoughts had only been centered on Casey and dreams of taking a shower with her.

How could he have screwed it up so badly? Dammit, Casey was right. He was allowing Norton and

Nan to call the shots. He'd let Norton talk him into a marriage because he'd played on Jack's loyalty to the older man. Nan showed gratitude and he felt guilty that he might be letting her down if he told her the truth about Casey. And while Norton looked healthy, he had no idea if that was nothing more than a facade for a fragile heart. He muttered curse after curse as he pounded his fist against the tile wall.

He stepped out of the shower and wrapped a towel around his hips and used another to dry his hair. He'd just stepped into his bedroom when he realized he wasn't alone.

"I must say you do look good wearing only a towel," Nan said. She was seated on the edge of his bed with her hands planted behind her to brace her body. The position showed her breasts to great advantage.

"I can't imagine you came up here to tell me it's time for dinner. I doubt I've been in the shower that long," he commented, opening a drawer and pulling out underwear.

"Dan said you told him to leave and find a place of his own," she said, sounding as if she couldn't believe he'd done so.

"That's right. Considering all you've done for him, he had no right to call you that. I doubt he's been looking for a job, and all he seems good for is working on his tan," Jack said scornfully. "You can't tell me he was out job-hunting while you two were in Kansas City."

She flushed. "He talked to some headhunters. There just weren't many opportunities there."

Jack leaned against his dresser. "Nan, he's using you. He has free room and board and no reason to get a job. How can you let him do that? Look at Casey. She's out there working and has a place of her own."

Nan stood up. "Dan is my business, not yours. He'll still be staying in the guest house, and next Monday he'll start work at the company. I'll see you at dinner."

Jack watched her leave. He felt as if he'd been sucker punched. But he wasn't about to stand still for more.

He pulled out the phone book and started making calls.

"HEY DOC CASEY, you've got a surprise out here!" Rachel the receptionist called out.

"And what a surprise," Ron said, grinning broadly as he passed Casey.

"Don't tell me, another kid who's going to up-chuck on me," she muttered, walking out to the reception desk. She stopped short at the sight of three five-gallon cartons in an ice-filled chest. "What is this?"

Rachel held up a square white envelope. "You tell us," she sang out, waving the envelope back and forth.

Casey snatched the envelope out of her hand and

tore it open. She pulled out the card and read the words. Then she read them again.

A carton for each year. Perhaps this will satisfy one small part of your hunger.

Love,
Jack

"What does it say?" Rachel demanded.

"Yeah, Casey, what does it say?" Greg asked, trying to look over Casey's shoulder. All he got was Casey's elbow in his stomach.

She tucked the card inside her shirt pocket. "It says we're going to have an ice-cream feast tonight." She noted the label on top of the carton that told her the cartons were filled with chocolate mint ice cream. First the candy, now the ice cream. Jack obviously remembered all the cravings she had when she was in the jungle. Too bad he didn't know about the thing she'd craved the most—him.

Rachel ran into the back and returned with bowls and spoons. "Next time ask him to send hot fudge, too," she asked.

"Fair enough." Casey laughed as she filled the bowls with the sweet treat.

And she couldn't stop smiling for the rest of night.

JACK WAS TIRED OF SHARING a nightly dinner with a smug Dan and quiet Nan. He had already heard Dan wasn't pulling his weight at work. Jack had brought it up to Nan, but she dismissed his comments, saying Dan would quickly settle in. Jack doubted it, but he didn't bother telling Nan that.

But every other day he sent Casey a surprise. After the chocolate mint ice cream, he had sent her a box of Milk Duds. Another day he had ordered her favorite pizza, which was followed up by a special delivery of a Chinese feast.

While he knew the deliveries were made, he heard nothing from Casey. His heart sank further with each passing day of silence.

"Is THERE ANY CHANCE of my getting a private office?" Dan asked that evening.

"I doubt it," Jack said grimly. "Those offices are for those who earn them."

"Give it some time, Dan," Nan advised. She looked irritated when the telephone rang. She got up and walked into the other room. She came back a moment later. "Jack, it's for you. He said his name is Greg." Her expression told him she was curious as to the man's identity.

Jack was equally curious as to why Greg would call him and quickly rose from the table. Within a few minutes, he was back, not saying anything about his call but quickly finishing his meal.

"I'm going out for a while," he announced after dinner.

Nan looked up, surprised by his words. "Out?"

"Just us, hey, cousin dear?" Dan quipped.

Despite Nan's look, Jack wasn't about to explain himself. Not with Dan sitting there. He simply turned away from the table and walked out.

Jack wasted no time in driving to the clinic. All that was on his mind was the need to find out what Greg wanted to tell him.

"Hi, there," Greg greeted him when he stepped inside. "I suggested here since I'm staying late to finish up some paperwork and I knew you wouldn't run into Casey. With her temper, I didn't think she should hear all of this."

"All of what?" Jack asked, following him down the hallway.

"Do you want some coffee?"

"No, thanks."

"Have a seat." Greg waved him toward a chair as he sat at the desk.

"Why did you call me?"

"You're the one sending her the gifts, right?"

Jack nodded.

"So you still love her."

"Of course I do!"

"Then why are you still with Nan when she and her father lied to you from the beginning?" Greg shouted. He took a deep breath. "Norton Xavier doesn't have a fatal heart condition. In fact, that heart attack he had was nothing more than a gastritis attack. It's not widely known, of course, because he wanted it that way. He wanted his daughter married and he saw you as the perfect husband. One he could control.

And when your 'sister' showed up, he saw another way to control you. Oceanview depends heavily on endowments from Xavier Electronics. Especially since their next dream is to build their own hospital. Norton Xavier pressures Gerald Montgomery to give Casey a cushy practice. Then, lo and behold, Gerald checks out Casey's qualifications and finds out she's married to Jonathon Larson." He shook his head at Jonathon's start of surprise. "Come on, Jack, you should have known someone could find out."

"So he knows his daughter isn't legally married and he hasn't done anything about it?" Jack was stunned.

"He has you running the company and that's what he wants. He knows that Nan wants to run it, but he doesn't want her in there, so he thought if he married her off by bribing her husband to take charge, he'd have things his way. As for your marriage, he probably figures he can talk you into a private ceremony later on. Norton is a power player, Jack." Greg stated what Jack knew but hadn't truly believed. "He likes things to go his way. He figured if Casey was at Oceanview he could use her as a bargaining chip. Once she had everything she could ever want, would you really want her to lose it—which she would if the two of you got back together. And you? You'd have the perfect wife, the perfect job, therefore, the perfect life. Norton would feel as if he'd done his job, and he could suddenly announce he felt much better and probably take off for Europe or something." He leaned back in his chair and waited as Jack assimilated all he just said.

"That son of a bitch," he said in a voice throbbing with anger. He clenched and unclenched his fists in his lap. Now he knew why Nan was eager to marry him. She knew he had no desire to run the company and she would be able to take over now or when they divorced. "How did you find out all of this?"

"I know a few people over there who heard just enough to let me put the pieces together. When I found out, I knew I had to call you and let you know what they had planned. Montgomery's a good doctor. The trouble is, he likes his social position and fat bank accounts more," Greg explained. "He knows Xavier's responsible for them, so he'll do whatever is necessary. You also have to figure that Nan has to know at least a part of this." He leaned forward. "So what will you do about it, Jack?"

Jack stood up. "Right a few wrongs." Seething, he strode out of the office intent on only one thing. At the door of the clinic, he paused and said over his shoulder, "I never thought I'd see the day I'd say this to you, Greg, but thanks."

JACK DROVE LIKE A MAN possessed. He made only one stop before driving to a small house situated across from the beach. He was relieved to see lights burning inside as he pulled up into the driveway. He walked up to the door and pushed the doorbell. He only hoped she wouldn't throw him out.

The door opened and Casey stood there just staring at him.

"I'm sorry," Jack said instantly.

"Sorry for what?" She didn't move away or invite him inside.

"Everything from the moment you showed up out here. You're right. I should have told Nan the truth, taken all the flack and then taken you off somewhere to work things out." He held out his hands, which were filled with two bouquets of bright yellow daffodils.

Casey didn't say anything. She stood there with her gaze centered on the colorful bouquets. Her lips quivered for a moment, but she made no move to take them. As if she'd made up her mind, she stepped back, silently inviting him inside.

"Would you like something to drink?" she asked quietly.

He shook his head. "I gave up alcohol."

A hint of a smile curved her lips. "Actually, I was talking more along the lines of iced tea."

"Fine."

She nodded and retreated to the kitchen. In a few moments, she returned with two ice-filled glasses of tea and a vase. She put the glasses down and took the flowers from him, carefully setting them in the vase. She sat down in a chair and curled her legs up under her.

"Why are you here?" she asked in a quiet voice.

Jack cradled the cold glass between his palms. It

seemed easier to look at it than her, but he knew he had to look at her as he explained.

"I found out tonight that everything was a lie." He stopped for a second, composing his thoughts. "Norton's heart attack, his so-called need for me to run the company, even your offer at Oceanview."

She sat quietly, allowing him to continue.

"You know, I thought I was doing the right thing. Norton was lying in that hospital bed, begging me to help him keep the company in the family.... He said he knew I was still in mourning for you, but I had to remember that it had been almost three years. I had to get on with my life. He said he couldn't think of a better man as his son-in-law than me. And Nan said she would do whatever was necessary to make her father's last days comfortable. She said we could consider it a marriage in name only, and after her father's death we could divorce if that's what I wanted."

"But there were times you got the idea she wanted more than a marriage in name only," she murmured.

He nodded again. "You got the raw end of the deal, Casey. You're my wife and I should have stood by you. I'd like to do that now, if you'll let me." He held her eyes with his. "I came here hoping we can talk all of this out and that maybe you'll give me a chance to make it all up to you."

Casey looked away. "Do you realize how much you've hurt me through all this?" she whispered.

"Yes and I deserve to be drawn and quartered for it."

"Actually, I'd come up with a much more painful punishment, but if that's what you want..." Her voice dropped off.

Jack could hear a faint trace of amusement in her voice. "You're going to make me jump through hoops here, aren't you?"

"Among other things." She leaned forward, resting her arm on her leg. "Jack, you can't expect to come back here and say you're sorry and I'll just welcome you back with open arms. Not after everything that's happened."

"No, I didn't expect that, but I did hope you'd give me a chance."

Casey stared at him for a long while and not once did he look away.

"It didn't take that night for me to know I still loved you," he went on. "I never stopped loving you. I just wasn't sure if you still loved me. Not when you went off to South America without thinking how I would feel about you being gone for so long," he said quietly. "You never asked me if I'd miss you or if it might be a better idea for you to stay, so we could hash out whatever problems we were having then. We didn't have a marriage, Casey. We were each living our own lives. We hadn't even tried to truly communicate with each other for so long I was afraid of losing you." The last two words came out as a whisper.

Casey got up and walked over to him. She kneeled down and settled her hands on his knees. "Why didn't you ever tell me?'' she murmured. ''Why didn't you tell me why you didn't want me to go?''

''I didn't think you'd care.''

Tears appeared in Casey's eyes and started trickling down her cheeks. She reached up to cup his face with her hands and pulled it down to hers. Her kiss was long and sweet. A silent reassurance that her feelings for him were strong.

Pretty soon it wasn't apparent if the moisture on their faces were from her tears or his.

''I've missed you,'' she whispered. ''I came back with the intention of fixing our marriage. In all my arrogance I was positive I could walk right in and everything would be normal because I said so. Finding out you'd left your position and moved—then that you were getting married—was a shock. It meant things were happening beyond my control. You had a good reason for what you did, and while it was probably more than a little illegal, your heart was in the right place.'' She whispered against his cheek. ''I thought posing as your sister would help. Instead, all it did was show me that you weren't the same man you were three years ago, and I already knew I wasn't the same woman. Then later on, I wanted to hate you...but you sent me ice cream and butter-toffee peanuts...and now you brought me daffodils.''

Jack wrapped his arms around her and pulled her up onto his lap. ''Does this mean you'll give me a chance?''

''By all rights I should tell you to go to hell,'' she

told him, cupping his face with her palms. "I should insist you get out of my life for good."

"But?" he asked, reading more into her gaze.

"But you're so damn cute and I love you. I'd be a fool to get rid of you. Besides, Nan doesn't deserve you."

Jack heaved a deep sigh of relief. "You won't regret it. I promise you." He hugged her tightly.

"Damn right I won't. Next time I get out the rusty scalpel," she threatened before kissing him.

Jack knew it didn't mean everything was clear, but it was definitely a beginning. He trailed his fingers across her bare knee, pushing her sundress farther up her leg.

"Professor, are you already thinking about seducing me?" Her question was a warm breath in his ear.

"Any objections?"

"None." She pulled his polo shirt out of his slacks waistband. "Just don't get the idea I'm easy."

He laughed and gasped at the same time when her fingers circled his nipple. "When did you pick up this crazy sense of humor?"

"You live in a jungle without modern conveniences and see if you don't come out with a sense of humor." She unzipped his slacks. "I don't know about you, but I think we'd be better off in a horizontal position."

Jack stood up, still keeping her in his arms. "Good idea."

Before Casey could say a word, he had her in the bedroom and stripped of her clothing.

"All I could think about was making love to you again," he rasped, nuzzling her neck. "I didn't want to leave here that morning."

"You sure acted like it." Her own hands were busy trailing up and down his spine. "I hated you that day."

"I hated me, too." He rubbed her belly in small circles that slowly grew larger, until he combed the thatch of brown hair at the apex of her thighs. He growled his pleasure when he found her already moist to the touch. He shifted his body so that he lay in the cradle of her thighs. "I never wanted anyone but you."

"I'm just glad you didn't marry Nan for love."

"We'll start from the beginning," he vowed as he thrust inside her. "All new." As her tight, moist center surrounded him, he was soon devoid of words. He could only go on sensation as he felt Casey enfold him with her arms and her body. "I love you, Casey Larson. I love you."

"You better, since I love you just as much." They were the last words he heard before he felt himself burst into flames. After that, he wasn't aware of anything.

CASEY WOKE UP FEELING marvelous. She rolled over and noticed Jack's face plopped against his pillow. She slid over to curl up against him. She thought about waking him up in a pleasurable way when she noticed his eyes were already open.

"This is the way it should be," he told her.

"Just remember that."

"Damn, I'm hungry."

She rose up over him. "For me?"

"For bacon and eggs. Hey!" He yelled when she started hitting him.

Jack pulled her down on him and all thoughts of breakfast were forgotten.

"I'VE GOT TO TALK TO NAN today. It has to be done, and it can't wait any longer."

Casey stilled at Jack's announcement. She held her tank top in her hand, now forgotten.

He had already pulled on his polo shirt. He walked over to her and put his arms around her. "I want us together, Casey. I want us to be a family."

"Babies?" she whispered.

"Think we can handle it?" he asked, rubbing his chin against the top of her head.

"After we straighten ourselves out, I bet we can take on the world," she said confidently, looping her arms around his waist.

"We'll just start on Nan and Norton." He kissed the top of her head. "How about I take you out for breakfast? Then I'll bring you back here before I meet with Nan and Norton."

She shook her head. "You forgot something, Professor. We're married, which means we do everything together. I'm going with you." She stepped out of his embrace and pulled on her tank top.

"I'm going to call Norton and ask him to meet me at the house," he said, reaching for the phone.

After the call and all through breakfast, Casey noticed Jack was distracted and knew it had to do with the upcoming confrontation. She had heard his half of the conversation with Norton and knew the man had demanded to know where he was. All Jack had told him was that he wanted to talk to him and Nan together in an hour and a half. After he got off the phone, he had held Casey tightly against him.

"Do you think you'll mind sharing the house with me?" he asked.

She pretended to think about it as she spread raspberry jam on her toast. "As long as you remember to put the toilet seat down and put the toothpaste tube top back on."

"Is there any reason why your soap smells like cinnamon?" He scratched his arm.

"It makes me smell good enough to eat," she purred, licking jam off her knife.

Jack closed his eyes and groaned. "Not now, Casey."

"But I did get your mind off other things, didn't I?" she teased.

He shook his head and chuckled. "Now I know you're nuts."

"But you love me, anyway," Casey said smugly.

She made sure to continue teasing him with fleeting

touches on his thigh as they drove back to Nan's house. By the time they arrived, Jack looked as if his blood pressure was ready to blow.

He stopped the car and turned to her. "I do love you, even if you have been trying to drive me insane for the past twenty minutes."

"It's just the beginning of what will happen when we get out of here," she promised as they climbed the steps to the front door. Before Jack could insert the key in the lock, the door opened, with Dan on the other side.

"Hey there, gorgeous," he greeted Casey. "Did you decide to keep big brother company?"

"Oh, Dan, you're such a dork," she murmured, following Jack into the house.

"Where have you been?" Casey could hear Nan's cry coming from the family room.

"Why the hell were you gone all night, worrying my baby?" Norton boomed next.

They turned to stare at Casey when she walked in and took a seat near the doorway.

"I was at Casey's," Jack explained.

Nan walked over to him and cupped her palm to his cheek. "Jack, I know you're unhappy with all that's happened lately, but all we had to do was talk about it." She frowned as she looked down at his arm. Her nose twitched. "Why do you smell like cinnamon?"

"If you want to talk, Nan, that's just what we're going to do. Please sit down. You too, Norton."

He glanced at Casey, who smiled and gave him a thumbs-up. He took a deep breath.

"I guess the only way to say this is to come right out."

"What are you trying to do to us, boy?" Norton demanded. "Are you finally going to tell the truth about Casey? That she isn't your sister. She's your wife." He waved away the exclamations from his daughter.

Jack didn't back away. "Yes, Casey's my wife. But I honestly did think she was dead. I had no idea she and an associate survived. They came back to the United States in time for Casey to show up at my wedding. The thing was—" he paused in his pacing "—I felt I owed you a great deal, Norton. You were worried about your company and about Nan. You felt I was perfect to step in and take care of everything. The only problem was you weren't as ill as you let on." He stared long and hard at the older man. "Gastritis isn't as serious as a heart attack. You were a lucky man. Too bad you felt you had to use it to reel me in. You all lied." He turned to Nan.

Her face flamed a bright red. "It's not what you think, Jack."

"It's not? Be honest. You went along with this because while your father saw me as heir apparent to Xavier Electronics and caretaker for his daughter, you saw me as an easy way to take over the company. You knew I didn't have the knowledge or desire to run it. Once you were secure, we could get a divorce, or as you said, we might decide to make it permanent."

"Make it permanent?" Dan echoed, looking at Nan. "You never said you thought about making it permanent!"

"That was one of the surprises, Dan," Casey spoke up. "Just like you pretending to be Nan's cousin when you're really her lover."

"What?" Norton shouted, glaring first at his daughter, then at Dan. "I should have known a pissant like you couldn't come from either side of the family."

"Daddy, it isn't what you think," Nan hastened to explain.

Jack spun around to stare at Casey. *Lover?* he mouthed.

She smiled and nodded. "All the signs were there if you cared to look."

Jack mouthed *I love you* while she blew him a kiss.

"All right, enough." He had to raise his voice. "Obviously, my marriage to Nan isn't valid and I guess it's a good thing it isn't."

"Do you realize what a scandal like this can do to us?" Norton demanded.

"Which? My wife coming back from the dead, your so-called heart attack or your daughter having a lover on the side?" Jack asked.

Norton groped for a chair and sat down heavily. He stared across the room at Casey.

"I gather his spending the night at your house didn't mean he slept on the couch," he sneered.

"Taking potshots at me won't make matters any better, Norton," she said. "Jack risked losing me because he felt he was helping you and Nan. It was a crazy situation and I didn't like it one bit, but I know my husband, and his loyalty should be respected, not played with." Her voice hardened.

"I'll take the blame for my part," Jack told Norton. "And I think it's best I resign from the company. I think I'm better off going back to teaching."

"But Jack—"

He cut off Nan's appeal with a shake of his head. "You have Dan. Maybe Norton will want to groom him." He turned back to Casey and held out his hand.

"Do you realize what you're doing?" Norton shouted at him.

Casey was the one to reply.

"Did you realize what you were doing when you played on his loyalty?" she said with quiet censure. "If anyone is to blame here, it's all three of you for lying. Somehow, I think you all deserve each other." She stood up and took Jack's hand.

"We never had a real honeymoon," Jack said to her as they walked out of the room, oblivious to the shouts and cries of outrage ringing through the room. "Do you think Greg and Ron could get along without you for a couple of weeks?"

"For a honeymoon, they will or they'll regret it."

She looped her arm through his. "May I make one suggestion?"

He stopped and drew her into his arms for a kiss. "Anything."

"I am willing to go anywhere in the world with you as long as it's not south of the border."

Jack's laughter drowned out the angry words still going on in the room they had just left. He picked her up in his arms and carried her out of the house and practically tossed her inside his car.

"Sweetheart, that won't be a problem. Besides, I doubt you'll have a chance to see much scenery, anyway."

And the Winner Is...
You!

...when you pick up these great titles
from our new promotion at your
favorite retail outlet this June!

Diana Palmer
The Case of the Mesmerizing Boss

Betty Neels
The Convenient Wife

Annette Broadrick
Irresistible

Emma Darcy
A Wedding to Remember

Rachel Lee
Lost Warriors

Marie Ferrarella
Father Goose

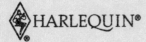 

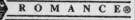

Once upon a time…

We were little girls dreaming of
handsome princes on white chargers…of
fairy godmothers…and of mountain castles
where we'd live happily ever after.

Now that we're all grown up,
Harlequin American Romance lets us
recapture those dreams in a brand-new
miniseries aimed at the little girl who still
lives on inside us. Join us for stories
based on some of the world's best-loved
fairy tales in

Once Upon a Kiss…

Watch for the next dreamy
fairy-tale romance:

WAKE ME WITH A KISS
by Emily Dalton
Available in July 1997

Once Upon a Kiss… At the heart
of every little girl's dream…and every
woman's fantasy…

FAIRY 3

It's hot…and it's out of control!

Beginning this spring, Temptation turns up the *heat*. Look for these bold, provocative, *ultra*sexy books!

#629 OUTRAGEOUS
by Lori Foster (April 1997)

#639 RESTLESS NIGHTS
by Tiffany White (June 1997)

#649 NIGHT RHYTHMS
by Elda Minger (Sept. 1997)

BLAZE: Red-hot reads—only from

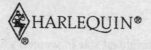

New York Times Bestselling Authors

JENNIFER BLAKE
JANET DAILEY
ELIZABETH GAGE

Three *New York Times* bestselling authors bring you three very sensuous, contemporary love stories—all centered around one magical night!

It is a warm, spring night and masquerading as legendary lovers, the elite of New Orleans society have come to celebrate the twenty-fifth anniversary of the Duchaise masquerade ball. But amidst the beauty, music and revelry, some of the world's most legendary lovers are in trouble....

Come midnight at this year's Duchaise ball, passion and scandal will be...

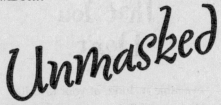

Unmasked

Revealed at your favorite retail outlet in July 1997.

<u>MIRA</u> **The brightest star in women's fiction**

HE SAID

♥

SHE SAID

Explore the mystery of male/female communication in this extraordinary new book from two of your favorite Harlequin authors.

Jasmine Cresswell and Margaret St. George bring you the exciting story of two romantic adversaries—each from their own point of view!

DEV'S STORY. CATHY'S STORY.
As he sees it. As she sees it.
Both sides of the story!

The heat is definitely on, and these two can't stay out of the kitchen!

Don't miss **HE SAID, SHE SAID.**
Available in July wherever Harlequin books are sold.

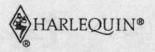

He changes diapers, mixes formula and
tells wonderful bedtime stories—he's

Mr. Mom

Three totally different stories of sexy, single
heroes each raising another man's child...
from three of your favorite authors:

MEMORIES OF THE PAST
by Carole Mortimer

THE MARRIAGE TICKET
by Sharon Brondos

TELL ME A STORY
by Dallas Schulze

Available this June wherever
Harlequin and Silhouette books are sold.

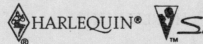 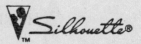